THE ANNOTATED SHAKESPEARE

Twelfth Night,
or, What You Will

William Shakespeare

Edited, fully annotated, and introduced by Burton Raffel

With an essay by Harold Bloom

THE ANNOTATED SHAKESPEARE

Yale University Press · New Haven and London

Harold Bloom, Introduction to *Twelfth Night,* copyright © 1987,
adapted and reprinted with permission of Chelsea House Publishers,
an imprint of Infobase Publishing.

Designed by Rebecca Gibb.
Set in Bembo type by The Composing Room of Michigan, Inc.
Printed in the United States of America by R. R. Donnelley & Sons.

Library of Congress Cataloging-in-Publication Data
Shakespeare, William, 1564–1616.
[Twelfth night]
Twelfth night, or, What you will / William Shakespeare ; edited, fully annotated,
and introduced by Burton Raffel ; with an essay by Harold Bloom.
p.   cm. — (The annotated Shakespeare)
Includes bibliographical references.
ISBN-13: 978-0-300-11563-5 (paperbound)
1. Survival after airplane accidents, shipwrecks, etc.—Drama.   2. Brothers
and sisters—Drama.   3. Mistaken identity—Drama.   4. Illyria—Drama.
5. Twins—Drama.   I. Raffel, Burton.   II. Bloom, Harold.   III. Title.
IV. Title: Twelfth night.   V. Title: What you will.
PR2837.A2R28 2007
822.3'3—dc22
2006036233

A catalogue record for this book is available from the British Library.

10 9 8 7 6 5 4 3 2 1

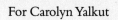

For Carolyn Yalkut

CONTENTS

O rsino's famous soliloquy, which opens the play, reads as
follows:

If music be the food of love, play on,
Give me excess of it, that surfeiting,
The appetite may sicken, and so die.
That strain again, it had a dying fall.
O it came o'er my ear, like the sweet sound
That breathes upon a bank of violets,
Stealing and giving odor. Enough, no more,
'Tis not so sweet now as it was before.
O spirit of love, how quick and fresh art thou,
That notwithstanding thy capacity
Receiveth as the sea, nought enters there,
Of what validity and pitch soe'er,
But falls into abatement and low price,
Even in a minute. So full of shapes is fancy
That it alone is high fantastical.

This was perfectly understandable, we must assume, to the mostly
very average persons who paid to watch Elizabethan plays. But

though much remains clear, who today can make full or entirely comfortable sense of the soliloquy? In this very fully annotated edition, I therefore present this passage, not in the bare form quoted above, but thoroughly supported by bottom-of-the-page notes:

> If music be the food of love, play on,
> Give me excess of it, that surfeiting,[1]
> The appetite[2] may sicken, and so die.
> That strain[3] again, it had a dying fall.[4]
> O it came o'er[5] my ear, like the sweet sound
> That breathes[6] upon a bank[7] of violets,
> Stealing[8] and giving[9] odor. Enough, no more,
> 'Tis not so sweet now as it was before.
> O spirit[10] of love, how quick and fresh[11] art thou,
> That notwithstanding[12] thy capacity
> Receiveth[13] as the sea,[14] nought enters there,
> Of what validity and pitch[15] soe'er,

1 that surfeiting = so that having had more than enough
2 desire
3 melody, tune
4 dying fall = languishing descent/sinking/cascading movement
5 came o'er = descended upon, passed over
6 exhales/blows softly
7 slope, bed
8 taking away ("gaining") from the flowers
9 bringing odor with it, as breezes do
10 (1) essential substance/principle/nature, (2) breath, movement of air, wind, (3) melody, music
11 quick and fresh = lively and refreshing/pure★
12 that notwithstanding = so that even though
13 capacity receiveth = ability to take things in absorbs such things
14 "Sea refuseth no water": *The Wordsworth Dictionary of Proverbs,* ed. G. L. Apperson (Hertfordshire: Wordsworth, 1993), 555a
15 validity and pitch = strength/force and from what height/how/at what angle thrown (n.b.: "pitch" as a musical term was also used in Shakespeare's time)

But falls into abatement and low price,[16]
Even in a minute. So full of shapes is fancy[17]
That it alone is high fantastical.[18]

Without full explanation of words that have over the years shifted in meaning, and usages that have been altered, neither the modern reader nor the modern listener is likely to be equipped for anything like full comprehension.

I believe annotations of this sort create the necessary bridges, from Shakespeare's four-centuries-old English across to ours. Some readers, to be sure, will be able to comprehend unusual, historically different meanings without any glosses. Those not familiar with the modern meaning of particular words will easily find clear, simple definitions in any modern dictionary. But most readers are not likely to understand Shakespeare's intended meaning, absent such glosses as I here offer.

My annotation practices have followed the same principles used in *The Annotated Milton,* published in 1999, and in my annotated editions of *Hamlet,* published (as the initial volume in this series) in 2003, *Romeo and Juliet* (published in 2004), and subsequent volumes in this series. Classroom experience has validated these editions. Classes of mixed upper-level undergraduates and graduate students have more quickly and thoroughly transcended language barriers than ever before. This allows the teacher, or a general reader without a teacher, to move more promptly and confidently to the nonlinguistic matters that have made Shakespeare and Milton great and important poets.

It is the inevitable forces of linguistic change, operant in all liv-

16 abatement and low price = diminishing and reduced worth/value
17 shapes is fancy=images/pictures is the imagination*
18 high fantastical = strongly/greatly/richly amorous inclination, love

ing tongues, which have inevitably created such wide degrees of obstacles to ready comprehension—not only sharply different meanings, but subtle, partial shifts in meaning which allow us to think we understand when, alas, we do not. Speakers of related languages like Dutch and German also experience this shifting of the linguistic ground. Like early Modern English (ca. 1600) and the Modern English now current, those languages are too close for those who know only one language, and not the other, to be readily able always to recognize what they correctly understand and what they do not. When, e.g., a speaker of Dutch says "Men kofer is kapot," a speaker of German will know that something belonging to the Dutchman is broken (kapot = "kaputt" in German, and men = "mein"). But without more linguistic awareness than the average person is apt to have, the German speaker will not identify "kofer" ("trunk" in Dutch) with "Körper"—a modern German word which means "physique, build, body." The closest word to "kofer" in modern German, indeed, is "Scrankkoffer," which is too large a leap for ready comprehension. Speakers of different Romance languages (French, Spanish, Italian), and all other related but not identical tongues, all experience these difficulties, as well as the difficulty of understanding a text written in their own language five, or six, or seven hundred years earlier. Shakespeare's English is not yet so old that it requires, like many historical texts in French and German, or like Old English texts —e.g., *Beowulf*—a modern translation. Much poetry evaporates in translation: language is immensely particular. The sheer *sound* of Dante in thirteenth-century Italian is profoundly worth preserving. So too is the sound of Shakespeare.

I have annotated prosody (metrics) only when it seemed truly necessary or particularly helpful. Readers should have no problem with the silent "e" in past participles (loved, returned, missed). Except in the few instances where modern usage syllabifies the "e," whenever an "e" in Shakespeare is *not* silent, it is marked "è." The notation used for prosody, which is also used in the explanation of Elizabethan pronunciation, follows the extremely simple form of my *From Stress to Stress: An Autobiography of English Prosody* (see "Further Reading," near the end of this book). Syllables with metrical stress are capitalized; all other syllables are in lowercase letters. I have managed to employ normalized Elizabethan spellings, in most indications of pronunciation, but I have sometimes been obliged to deviate, in the higher interest of being understood.

I have annotated, as well, a limited number of such other matters, sometimes of interpretation, sometimes of general or historical relevance, as have seemed to me seriously worthy of inclusion. These annotations have been most carefully restricted: this is not intended to be a book of literary commentary. It is for that reason that the glossing of metaphors has been severely restricted. There is almost literally no end to discussion and/or analysis of metaphor, especially in Shakespeare. To yield to temptation might well be to double or triple the size of this book—and would also change it from a historically oriented language guide to a work of an unsteadily mixed nature. In the process, I believe, neither language nor literature would be well or clearly served.

Where it seemed useful, and not obstructive of important textual matters, I have modernized spelling, including capitalization. Spelling is not on the whole a basic issue, but punctuation and lineation must be given high respect. The Folio uses few exclamation marks or semicolons, which is to be sure a matter of the conventions of a very different era. Still, our modern preferences cannot be lightly substituted for what is, after a fashion, the closest thing to a Shakespeare manuscript we are likely ever to have. We do not know whether these particular seventeenth-century printers, like most of that time, were responsible for question marks, commas, periods, and, especially, all-purpose colons, or whether these particular printers tried to follow their hand-written sources. Nor do we know if those sources, or what part thereof, might have been in Shakespeare's own hand. But in spite of these equivocations and uncertainties, it remains true that, to a very considerable extent, punctuation tends to result from just how the mind responsible for that punctuating *hears* the text. And twenty-first-century minds have no business, in such matters, overruling seventeenth-century ones. Whoever the compositors were, they were more or less Shakespeare's contemporaries, and we are not.

Accordingly, when the original printed text uses a comma, we are being signaled that *they* (whoever "they" were) heard the text, not coming to a syntactic stop, but continuing to some later stopping point. To replace commas with editorial periods is thus risky and on the whole an undesirable practice. (The play's dramatic action, to be sure, may require us, for twenty-first-century readers, to highlight what four-hundred-year-old punctuation standards may not make clear—and may even, at times, misrepresent.)

When the printed text has a colon, what we are being signaled is that *they* heard a syntactic stop—though not necessarily or even usually the particular kind of syntactic stop we associate, today, with the colon. It is therefore inappropriate to substitute editorial commas for original colons. It is also inappropriate to employ editorial colons when *their* syntactic usage of colons does not match ours. In general, the closest thing to *their* syntactic sense of the colon is our (and their) period.

The printed interrogation (question) marks, too, merit extremely respectful handling. In particular, editorial exclamation marks should very rarely be substituted for interrogation marks.

It follows from these considerations that the movement and sometimes the meaning of what we must take to be Shakespeare's play will at times be different, depending on whose punctuation we follow, *theirs* or our own. I have tried, here, to use the printed seventeenth-century text as a guide to both *hearing* and *understanding* what Shakespeare wrote.

Since the original printed texts (there not being, as there never are for Shakespeare, any surviving manuscripts) are frequently careless as well as self-contradictory, I have been relatively free with the wording of stage directions—and in some cases have added brief directions, to indicate who is speaking to whom. I have made no emendations; I have necessarily been obliged to make choices. Textual decisions have been annotated when the differences between or among the original printed texts seem either marked or of unusual interest.

In the interests of compactness and brevity, I have employed in my annotations (as consistently as I am able) a number of stylistic and typographical devices:

- The annotation of a single word does not repeat that word

- The annotation of more than one word repeats the words being annotated, which are followed by an equals sign and then by the annotation; the footnote number in the text is placed after the last of the words being annotated

- In annotations of a single word, alternative meanings are usually separated by commas; if there are distinctly different ranges of meaning, the annotations are separated by arabic numerals inside parentheses—(1), (2), and so on; in more complexly worded annotations, alternative meanings expressed by a single word are linked by a forward slash, or solidus: /

- Explanations of textual meaning are not in parentheses; comments about textual meaning are

- Except for proper nouns, the word at the beginning of all annotations is in lower case

- Uncertainties are followed by a question mark, set in parentheses: (?)

- When particularly relevant, "translations" into twenty-first-century English have been added, in parentheses

- Annotations of repeated words are *not* repeated. Explanations of the *first* instance of such common words are followed by the sign ★. Readers may easily track down the first annotation, using the brief Finding List at the back of the book. Words with entirely separate meanings are annotated *only* for meanings no longer current in Modern English.

The most important typographical device here employed is the sign ★ placed after the first (and only) annotation of words and phrases occurring more than once. There is an alphabetically arranged listing of such words and phrases in the Finding List at the back of the book. The Finding List contains no annotations but simply gives the words or phrases themselves and the numbers of the relevant act, the scene within that act, and the foot-note number within that scene for the word's first occurrence.

INTRODUCTION

Those in search of entertainment usually prefer to know, more or less in advance, what sort of entertainment they have chosen and for which they are paying. Those who attend a performance of *The Most Excellent and Lamentable Tragedy of Romeo and Juliet* neither expect nor would probably readily accept a song-and-dance farce. Similarly, a performance of *The Comical History of the Merchant of Venice, or Otherwise Called the Jew of Venice* is not likely to be "lamentable tragedy," though the unusually long and remarkably detailed title suggests that this "comical history," too, is not of the song-and-dance variety.

Shakespeare's plays have been in constant performance for four hundred years and more; we commonly shorten their familiar and well-understood titles. *Romeo and Juliet* and *The Merchant of Venice* are all we have come to need. But *Twelfth Night* comes to us (uniquely, for Shakespeare) along with a second, alternative title. This alternative, *What You Will,* may well have been the original title and could have been changed (we do not know) in order to avoid conflict with John Marston's play by that name. Though it was written about 1600, just before *Hamlet, Twelfth Night* first appeared in print in the 1623 Folio, with the alternative title attached, and there it has remained. We assume that Shakespeare so intended, though there is no evidence, just as there is none to contradict the assumption.

The paired titles are particularly important in determining three major issues: (1) the probable date of composition, (2) the probable date and place of first performance, and (3) authorial intent—that is, since we have only the text, and not a shred of external information as to what Shakespeare intended, the *play's* intentions. *Twelfth Night* clearly alludes to the Twelfth Day of Christmas, the sixth day of January (also known as Epiphany). This an important day in the Christian year, deeply grounded in English as well as European history. Indeed, the Elizabethans' perception of the calendar was governed by such religious observances rather than by mere days of the month: the eighth day of January, for example, was more likely to be referred to as "two days after Epiphany."

But all attempts to link the religious aspects of the holiday to Shakespeare's *Twelfth Night* have failed. Even apart from the plainly secular nature of the text, this is because the Twelfth Day of Christmas had become a universally joyous and sometimes a riotously liberated celebration, just as Christmas itself (historically of pagan origin) had "continued to be a great secular feast as well as a religious one."[1] So, too, purported links between court observance of the holiday and the play's first performance have been unconvincing in the extreme. Leslie Hotson's study (cited in "Further Reading") is a gold mine of widely assorted cultural and historical data, most interestingly recorded. However, it does not establish any linkage between its fascinating data and Shakespeare's play. It is demonstrably true that, in 1594, "Twelfth Night was celebrated at Court by dancing which continued till 1 o'clock after midnight, the Queen [Elizabeth] being seated on a high throne, and next to her chair the Earl of Essex with whom she often devised [conversed] in sweet and favorable manner."[2] But such evidence is linked only to the holiday and not to our play.

Still, although festive comedy is not all the play is concerned with, the nature of Twelfth Night celebrations is indeed very like the festive comedy of *Twelfth Night.* For example, in the universities of Europe, "Only on Twelfth-night were mummers [mimes] allowed within the sacred precincts of the college."[3] "The Feast of Epiphany, or Twelfth Night, was the most important masquing [masquerading] night, commemorating the recognition of Christ's birth by the Three Magi."[4] When John Milton attacked King Charles's distinctly heroic calm, as displayed on the scaffold prior to his execution, he described the king's actions as a performance, "a masking scene . . . [with] quaint emblems and devices, begged from the old pageantry of some Twelfthnight's entertainment at Whitehall [the court]."[5]

It is no accident, accordingly, that *Twelfth Night's* important "clown" role is assigned to a character named Feste. Nor is it accidental that the social role of children was much enlarged on Twelfth Night, "probably the greatest festival of the year. . . . A miniature [painted at the end of the fifteenth century] depicts the first episode of the festival . . . [and] record[s] the moment when, in accordance with tradition, it was a child who shared out the Twelfth-cake. . . . The playing of this part by the child implies his presence in the midst of the adults during the long hours of the Twelfth Night vigil."[6] All the same, the Twelfth day of Christmas is neither mentioned nor in any direct way involved in the play.

The alternative title, *What You Will,* makes no specific reference to any external event. Here, too, linkages have been asserted, but never successfully maintained. Yet the less allusive second title throws perhaps as much light on the play as does the first title. To better understand the significance of *What You Will,* it may help to consider the following list of twenty dramatic titles, presented in strictly alphabetical order:

1. *All's Well That Ends Well*
2. *Anything Goes*
3. *As You Like It*
4. *The Comedy of Errors*
5. *A Dangerous Maid*
6. *Everybody's Doing It*
7. *I'd Rather Be Right*
8. *Let's Face It*
9. *Merrie England*
10. *Much Ado about Nothing*
11. *A Night Out*
12. *Nymph Errant*
13. *Oh I Say*
14. *On Your Toes*
15. *Out of This World*
16. *Sigh No More*
17. *Tell Me More*
18. *Wake Up and Dream*
19. *Yeomen of the Guard*
20. *You Never Know*

Of these twenty more or less similar titles, only numbers 1, 3, 4, and 10 are by Shakespeare. The others are all what we call "musical comedy."[7]

Yet as this list of titles illustrates, musical comedy tends to be based on much the same spirit as that in which most of Shakespeare's comedies were written, though the literary level is generally a good deal reduced. The text of *Twelfth Night* makes it plain that Shakespeare had other things than sheer "comedy" on his mind. Splendid though Cole Porter's work may be, no one would argue that he was capable of (or interested in) writing anything even remotely like *Hamlet, Macbeth,* or *Othello*.[8] After all, there are three hundred and some years between the theater that gave birth to the non-Shakespearean plays on this list and the theater of Elizabethan England. But the gaiety and abandon of fifteen of the other sixteen plays remains both remarkably similar and distinctly significant. (William Gilbert and Arthur Sullivan's *Yeomen of the Guard* is not particularly cheerful; neither is Shakespeare, at times, even in so-called comedies.) The spirit of *What You Will* needs and will support, I think, no further underlining than this.

Twelfth Night is an extraordinarily bold play, ambitious in ways that Shakespeare's earlier comedies cannot fully match. I have been stressing the comedic sides of the play, which are not hard to find. *Twelfth Night* is indeed brilliantly merry, and its poetry is unmatchable. The soliloquy beginning "If music be the food of love, play on," words that introduce the play, is justly and universally celebrated. But there are a good many pointed, rather "darker" sides to *Twelfth Night*. Having been delinquent in his duties, Feste is warned that his mistress, Olivia, "will hang thee for thy absence." "Let her hang me," he replies, and immediately adds, "He that is well hanged in this world needs to fear no colors" (1.5.4–5). Some footnoting may clarify the keen pointedness of Feste's remarks. For a man to be "well hung" then meant exactly what it means today—that is, to be genitally well endowed. This is force-ful, though hardly subversive. But "colors" meant a number of things, some innocuous, some not: (1) enemies, (2) those who wear collars ("authority"), or those who have the "colors/ap-pearances" of authority, and (3) the hangman's noose, which was understood (and freely employed) as the ultimate enforcer of au-thority. Authority was then a good deal more important, and more strenuously insisted upon, than it usually is today; those who in any way resisted authority (also referred to as "order") were seen as dangerously evil. To be "disorderly" was not a trivial of-fense and was frequently a mortal one. A few lines farther along, Feste notes that "Many a good hanging prevents a bad marriage" (1.5.17). Again, this has a sexual thrust, but it is also an exten-sion of the antisocial coloration just noted. Clowns had social li-cense, up to a point; Feste's bluntness approaches long-standing and profoundly respected boundaries.

Nor is Feste the only character to voice doubts about the fab-ric of society. Feste is a clown and therefore off (or outside) the social scale. Doubts about society, from such a character, are of less weight, and less surprising, than such doubts emanating from people notably higher in rank. (Everyone in Elizabethan England had a ranking; it was a profoundly hierarchical world.) Maria is a "gentlewoman," the now-obsolete female counterpart of "gen-tleman"; neither designation was a casual affair, and both designa-tions opened a wide variety of social doors. We do not think of literacy as one such door, but most Elizabethans, and especially the great majority who worked for a living, were not literate. Maria is so manifestly literate that she can quite successfully ape her mistress's handwriting, not to mention her literary style. Maria is her lady's chambermaid, and though a gentlewoman is considerably lower on the social scale than a "lady," the personal servant of a woman of Olivia's wealth (which is considerable) and standing (Olivia is a countess) is not an ordinary "servant." Even the much-despised Malvolio, who in truth works hard at earning others' dislike, is a gentleman: neither he nor Maria could think of "marrying up," as both do think (and one of whom successfully does), if either were at the nether end of the personal-service scale.

Yet Maria (in the best Shakespearean tradition) has her eyes open and can observe that Malvolio is "villainously" yellow-stockinged and cross-gartered, "like a pedant that keeps a school" (3.2.66–67). There were then no state-supported schools; church-based education formed a significant part of what schooling was available. The church itself was of such social importance that people were obliged by law to attend services and were subject to punishment for failing to do so. "Pedant" was then, as it is today, a negatively flavored term, so Maria is plainly not speaking Feste-like heresies. But she has a consistently direct tongue: as she says of Malvolio, he is not a Puritan "but a time-pleaser" and, to boot, "an affectioned ass" (2.3.137). These are the sorts of spices that properly season so ripe a Shakespearean brew.

We might not expect a rowdy, carousing knight to voice sentiments sharply aimed at the social fabric, and Sir Toby does not do so. But neither does he accept all of society's values. When Maria scolds him, observing that "you must confine yourself within the modest limits of order," he assures her that he will "confine [as he here uses the word, it means "clothe"] myself no finer than I am. These clothes are good enough to drink in, and so be these boots too" (1.3.9–11). Like virtually everyone else in the play, Sir Toby deals bluntly with Malvolio: "Dost thou think, because thou art virtuous, there shall be no more cakes and ale?" (2.3.108–9).

Most of *Twelfth Night*'s spice, however, comes to us from Viola.

Involuntarily freed from the constraining bonds of young womanhood, first by calamity and then by the necessity of pretending to be male, her tongue is magnificently free. Sent as love's messenger to Countess Olivia, Viola does not know which of the two gentlewomen she faces, Olivia or Maria, is the one to address. Without identifying herself, Olivia advises Viola to speak to her. Viola replies: "Most radiant, exquisite, and unmatchable beauty— I pray you, tell me if this be the lady of the house, for I never saw her. I would be loath to cast away my speech, for besides that it is excellently well penned, I have taken great pains to con it" (1.5.159–63). Witty, not to say hilarious, this is also remarkably un-self-conscious. The audience of course is fully aware that this is one lovely young woman speaking, in disguise, to another lovely young woman—a device common enough on the Elizabethan stage, but here made unusually pungent. Though audiences respond to Olivia, lines like these make Viola the emotional center of the play.

Later in the scene, Olivia challenges her: "Yet you began rudely. What are you? What would you?" Viola's response drops away from badinage, touching deep, powerful chords: "The rudeness that hath appeared in me have I learned from my entertainment [reception]. What I am, and what I would, are as secret as maidenhead. To your ears, divinity. To any other's, profanation" (lines 197–202). Although Olivia responds favorably, sending Maria and her other attendants out of the room, she cannot respond so deeply as we do. She is not in on the secret, and we are. Further, Shakespeare's Elizabethan audiences, as compared to modern ones, placed considerably higher value on the three key words of Viola's speech: maidenhead (virginity), divinity (the Deity), and profanation (desecration, pollution of that which is sacred). To better appreciate Viola's intense solemnity, imagine this speech, spoken by some different character, in, say, *Othello*. Or *Macbeth*. Or *King Lear.* There would be no discordance, no jarring of tone. In the comedic setting of *Twelfth Night,* the speech reverberates like a church organ. To put it differently, this is not comedy as it has usually been exhibited on any stage, anywhere, or at any time.

Notes

1. E. K. Chambers, *English Literature at the Close of the Middle Ages,* rev. ed. (New York: Oxford University Press, 1947), 84.
2. G. B. Harrison, ed., *The Elizabethan Journals: Being a Record of Those Things Most Talked of During the Years, 1591–1597,* abridged ed., 2 vols. (New York: Doubleday Anchor, 1965), 1:221.
3. Hastings Rashdall, *The Universities of Europe in the Middle Ages,* rev. ed., ed. F. M. Powicke, 3 vols. (Oxford: Oxford University Press, 1936), 3:424.
4. Patricia Fumerton, *Cultural Aesthetics: Renaissance Literature and the Practice of Social Ornament* (Chicago: University of Chicago Press, 1991), 155.
5. Fumerton, *Cultural Aesthetics,* 15.
6. Philippe Ariès, *Centuries of Childhood: A Social History of Family Life,* trans. Robert Baldick (New York: Random House, 1962), 73–74.
7. Cole Porter (2, 8, 11, 12, 15, 18, and 20), George Gershwin (5, 17), Richard Rodgers and Lorenz Hart (7, 14), Jerome Kern (13), Irving Berlin (6), Noël Coward (16), William Gilbert and Arthur Sullivan (19), and Edward German and Basil Hood (9).
8. Porter's *Kiss Me Kate* is a splendid reworking of Shakespeare's *Taming of the Shrew,* portions of which have been drawn on both for the musical comedy's title and some of its lyrics. Stephen Sondheim, considerably more "literary" than Porter, writes more "crossover" than "standard" popular theatricals— more like, say, the work of John Adams or Philip Glass, who are classified as "classical."

SOME ESSENTIALS OF THE SHAKESPEAREAN STAGE

The Stage

- There was no *scenery* (backdrops, flats, and so on).

- Compared to today's elaborate, high-tech productions, the Elizabethan stage had few *on-stage* props. These were mostly handheld: a sword or dagger, a torch or candle, a cup or flask. Larger props, such as furniture, were used sparingly.

- Costumes (some of which were upper-class castoffs, belonging to the individual actors) were elaborate. As in most premodern and very hierarchical societies, clothing was the distinctive mark of who and what a person was.

- What the actors *spoke,* accordingly, contained both the dramatic and narrative material we have come to expect in a theater (or movie house) and (1) the setting, including details of the time of day, the weather, and so on, and (2) the occasion. The *dramaturgy* is thus very different from that of our own time, requiring much more attention to verbal and gestural matters. Strict realism was neither intended nor, under the circumstances, possible.

- There was *no curtain*. Actors entered and left via doors in the back of the stage, behind which was the "tiring-room," where actors put on or changed their costumes.

- In *public theaters* (which were open-air structures), there was no *lighting;* performances could take place only in daylight hours.
- For *private* theaters, located in large halls of aristocratic houses, candlelight illumination was possible.

The Actors

- Actors worked in *professional,* for-profit companies, sometimes organized and owned by other actors, and sometimes by entrepreneurs who could afford to erect or rent the company's building. Public theaters could hold, on average, two thousand playgoers, most of whom viewed and listened while standing. Significant profits could be and were made. Private theaters were smaller, more exclusive.

- There was *no director.* A book-holder/prompter/props manager, standing in the tiring-room behind the backstage doors, worked from a text marked with entrances and exits and notations of any special effects required for that particular script. A few such books have survived. Actors had texts only of their own parts, speeches being cued to a few prior words. There were few and often no rehearsals, in our modern use of the term, though there was often some coaching of individuals. Since Shakespeare's England was largely an oral culture, actors learned their parts rapidly and retained them for years. This was *repertory* theater, repeating popular plays and introducing some new ones each season.

- *Women* were not permitted on the professional stage. Most female roles were acted by *boys;* elderly women were played by grown men.

The Audience

- London's professional theater operated in what might be called a "red-light" district, featuring brothels, restaurants, and the kind of *open-air entertainment* then most popular, like bear-baiting (in which a bear, tied to a stake, was set on by dogs).

- A theater audience, like most of the population of Shakespeare's England, was largely made up of illiterates. Being able to read and write, however, had nothing to do with intelligence or concern with language, narrative, and characterization. People attracted to the theater tended to be both extremely verbal and extremely volatile. Actors were sometimes attacked, when the audience was dissatisfied; quarrels and fights were relatively common. Women were regularly in attendance, though no reliable statistics exist.

- Drama did not have the cultural esteem it has in our time, and plays were not regularly printed. Shakespeare's often appeared in book form, but not with any supervision or other involvement on his part. He wrote a good deal of nondramatic poetry as well, yet so far as we know he did not authorize or supervise any work of his that appeared in print during his lifetime.

- Playgoers, who had paid good money to see and hear, plainly gave dramatic performances careful, detailed attention. For some closer examination of such matters, see Burton Raffel, "Who Heard the Rhymes and How: Shakespeare's Dramaturgical Signals," *Oral Tradition* 11 (October 1996): 190–221, and Raffel, "Metrical Dramaturgy in Shakespeare's Earlier Plays," *CEA Critic* 57 (Spring–Summer 1995): 51–65.

Twelfth Night, or, What You Will

CHARACTERS (DRAMATIS PERSONAE)

Orsino[1] (Duke of Ilyria)
Sebastian (Viola's brother)
Antonio (sea captain, Sebastian's friend)
Sea Captain (Viola's friend)
Sir Toby Belch (Olivia's uncle)
Sir Andrew Aguecheek
Malvolio (Olivia's steward)
Curio, Valentine (the Duke's attendants)
Fabian (Olivia's servant)
Feste, a clown (Olivia's servant)
Olivia (a countess)
Viola[2] (Sebastian's sister)
Maria (Olivia's chambermaid)
Lords, Sailors, a Priest, Officers, Musicians, and Attendants

1 orSEEno
2 VIEohLA or VAYohLA

Act I

Duke Orsino's palace

ENTER DUKE ORSINO, CURIO, AND OTHER LORDS,
AND MUSICIANS

Orsino If music be the food of love, play on,
    Give me excess of it, that surfeiting,[1]
    The appetite[2] may sicken, and so die.
    That strain[3] again, it had a dying fall.[4]
    O it came o'er[5] my ear, like the sweet sound   5
    That breathes upon a bank[6] of violets,
    Stealing[7] and giving[8] odor. Enough, no more,
    'Tis not so sweet now as it was before.

---

1 that surfeiting = so that having had more than enough
2 desire
3 melody, tune
4 dying fall = languishing descent/sinking/cascading movement/cadence
5 came o'er = descended upon, passed over
6 breathes upon a bank = blows upon a slope/bed
7 taking away ("gaining") from the flowers
8 bringing odor with it, as breezes do

O spirit[9] of love, how quick and fresh[10] art thou,
10 That notwithstanding[11] thy capacity
Receiveth[12] as the sea,[13] nought enters there,
Of what validity and pitch[14] soe'er,
But falls into abatement and low price,[15]
Even in a minute. So full of shapes is fancy[16]
15 That it alone is high fantastical.[17]

Curio Will you[18] go hunt, my lord?
Orsino   What, Curio?
Curio The hart.[19]
Orsino   Why, so I do, the noblest that I have.
O when mine eyes did see Olivia first,
Methought she purged[20] the air of pestilence.[21]
20 That instant was I turned into a hart,
And my desires, like fell[22] and cruel hounds,
E'er since pursue me.

---

9 (1) essential substance/principle/nature, (2) breath, movement of air, wind,
   (3) melody, music
10 quick and fresh = lively/eager/ refreshing, pure★
11 that notwithstanding = so that even though
12 capacity receiveth = ability to take things in absorbs such things
13 "Sea refuseth no water" (*The Wordsworth Dictionary of Proverbs*, ed. G. L.
   Apperson [London: Wordsworth, 1993], 555a)
14 validity and pitch = strength/force and from what height/how/at what
   angle thrown (N.B.:"pitch" as a musical term was also used in Shakespeare's
   time)
15 abatement and low price = diminishing and reduced worth/value
16 the imagination★
17 high fantastical = strongly/greatly/richly amorous
18 will you = do you wish to
19 stag
20 cleansed, purified
21 (1) disease (especially plague), (2) wickedness, evil conduct, harmfulness
22 savage, ruthless

ENTER VALENTINE

How now,[23] what news from her?

Valentine So please[24] my lord, I might not[25] be admitted,

But from her handmaid[26] do return this answer:

The element[27] itself, till seven years' heat,[28]   25

Shall not behold her face at ample[29] view.

But like a cloistress[30] she will veilèd walk,

And water once a day her chamber round[31]

With eye-offending brine.[32] All this to season[33]

A brother's dead love, which she would[34] keep fresh   30

And lasting in her sad remembrance.[35]

Orsino   O, she that hath a heart of that fine frame[36]

To pay this debt of love but[37] to a brother,

How will she love, when the rich golden shaft[38]

Hath killed the flock[39] of all affections else[40]   35

23 how now = what's up ("what?")★
24 so please = may it please (polite convention)
25 I might not = I was not able to (the modern distinction between "can" and
   "may" is not applicable)
26 chambermaid, personal servant (i.e., Maria)
27 (1) sky, air, sun, (2) elements
28 warmth, operation, movement ("seasons")
29 full, complete
30 nun
31 all over/about, in all directions
32 salt ("tears")
33 alleviate, embalm, preserve
34 wishes/wants to
35 reMEMberANCE
36 constitution, nature, structure
37 just, only
38 i.e., Cupid's love arrow
39 band, company
40 affections else = other emotions/feelings/passions

That live in her? When liver,[41] brain, and heart,
These sovereign thrones,[42] are all supplied,[43] and filled
Her sweet perfections[44] with one self king?[45]
Away[46] before me, to sweet beds of flowers,
Love-thoughts lie[47] rich, when canopied with bowers.[48]

EXEUNT[49]

41 the site/stimulator of sexual desire★
42 sovereign thrones = supreme/highest powers/authorities
43 completed, furnished, provided for
44 filled her sweet perfections = her sweet perfections are filled
45 self king = sole/single ruler (i.e., love)
46 go
47 rest, lie down
48 canopied with bowers = covered/sheltered by overarching branches
49 they leave (Latin plural of "exit")★

SCENE 2

The seacoast

ENTER VIOLA, A CAPTAIN, AND SAILORS

Viola   What country, friends, is this?

Captain This is Illyria,[1] lady.

Viola   And what should I do[2] in Illyria?

My brother he is in Elysium.[3]

Perchance[4] he is not drowned. What think you sailors?   5

Captain It is perchance[5] that you yourself were saved.

Viola   O my poor brother, and so perchance may he be.

Captain True madam, and to comfort you with chance,[6]

Assure yourself,[7] after our ship did split,

When you, and those poor[8] number saved with you   10

Hung on our driving[9] boat, I saw your brother,

Most provident[10] in peril, bind[11] himself

(Courage and hope both teaching him the practice),

To a strong mast that lived[12] upon the sea,

Where like Arion[13] on the dolphin's back,   15

---

1 ancient realm on the eastern coast of the Adriatic Sea (ilLEAReeAH)

2 should I do = ought I do, am I doing

3 Greek mythology: residence of the blessed after death (my BROther HE is IN eLEEzeeUM)

4 perhaps*

5 by chance/accident (i.e., a pun on the literal meaning)

6 (1) fortune, luck, (2) accident ("that which can happen/occur")

7 assure yourself = be certain that

8 small, few

9 drifting

10 capable of foresight

11 fasten, tie

12 floated, survived

13 poet thrown into the sea and saved by a dolphin, which had heard and been charmed by his singing, and took him on its back (aWRYun)

I saw him hold[14] acquaintance with the waves
So long as I could see.

Viola   For saying so, there's gold.
Mine own escape unfoldeth[15] to my hope
20   (Whereto thy speech serves for authority)[16]
The like[17] of him. Know'st thou this country?

Captain Ay madam, well, for I was bred[18] and born
Not three hours' travel from this very[19] place.

Viola   Who governs here?

25 *Captain* A noble duke, in nature as in name.

Viola   What is his name?

Captain Orsino.

Viola   Orsino. I have heard my father name him.
He was a bachelor then.

30 *Captain* And so is now, or was so very late,[20]
For but a month ago I went from hence,
And then 'twas fresh in murmur[21] (as you know,
What great ones do the less[22] will prattle[23] of)
That he did seek the love of fair[24] Olivia.

35 *Viola*   What's she?

Captain A virtuous maid,[25] the daughter of a count[26]

14 maintain/keep/preserve his
15 opens
16 (1) authorization, (2) judgment, opinion
17 the like = for the same
18 raised, brought up
19 actual ("genuine")★
20 recently★
21 rumor
22 less great (commoners)
23 chatter
24 beautiful, pleasing, agreeable★
25 virgin
26 earl; the title is often used for dukes as well

That died some twelvemonth since, then leaving her
In the protection of his son, her brother,
Who shortly also died. For whose dear love
(They say) she hath abjured[27] the sight   40
And company[28] of men.

Viola   O that I served that lady,
And might not be delivered to[29] the world
Till I had made mine own occasion mellow[30]
What my estate[31] is.

Captain   That were hard to compass,[32]   45
Because she will admit no kind of suit,
No, not the Duke's.

Viola   There is a fair behavior[33] in thee, captain,
And though that[34] nature with a beauteous wall[35]
Doth oft close in[36] pollution,[37] yet of thee   50
I will[38] believe thou hast a mind that suits[39]
With this thy fair and outward character.[40]
I prithee[41] (and I'll pay thee bounteously)[42]

27 renounced, forsworn
28 companionship, association with
29 delivered to = sent into, surrendered, yielded
30 occasion mellow = opportunity/circumstances★ mature ("become clear")
31 condition, standing ("worldly fortune")★
32 contrive, manage
33 demeanor, bearing ("manners")
34 though that = although
35 exterior, outside ("appearance")
36 surround, contain
37 impurity, uncleanness, defilement
38 wish to
39 fits
40 nature, appearance
41 pray you = request/ask of you★
42 generously, amply

Conceal me what I am, and be my aid[43]
55   For such disguise as haply[44] shall become
The form of my intent.[45] I'll serve this Duke,
Thou shall[46] present me as an eunuch to him:
It may be worth thy pains. For I can sing,
And speak to him in many sorts of music
60   That will allow[47] me very worth[48] his service.
What else may hap[49] to time I will commit,[50]
Only shape thou thy silence to my wit.[51]

Captain Be you his eunuch, and your mute I'll be,[52]
When my tongue blabs,[53] then let mine eyes not see.
65 *Viola*   I thank thee. Lead[54] me on.

EXEUNT

43 support, help, assistance
44 perhaps★
45 form of my intent = shape / mode / pattern of my purpose / plan
46 must
47 prove, give
48 very worth = genuine value in / to
49 occur, happen
50 entrust to you
51 mind★
52 i.e., just as the "man" you pretend to be is a castrated man ("eunuch"), so too
    I will be like a dumb / mute man, incapable of speaking to betray you
53 babbles, betrays
54 guide, conduct

SCENE 3

Olivia's house

ENTER SIR TOBY BELCH AND MARIA

Sir Toby What a plague[1] means my niece, to take the death of
her brother thus? I am sure care's[2] an enemy to life.

Maria By my troth,[3] Sir Toby, you must come in earlier a'
nights. Your cousin,[4] my lady, takes great exceptions[5] to your
ill hours.   5

Sir Toby Why, let her except, before excepted.[6]

Maria Ay, but you must confine yourself within the modest[7]
limits of order.

Sir Toby Confine? I'll confine myself no finer[8] than I am. These
clothes are good enough to drink in, and so be these boots   10
too. An[9] they be not, let them hang themselves in their own
straps.[10]

Maria That quaffing[11] and drinking will undo you. I heard my
lady talk of it yesterday. And of a foolish knight that you

---

1 what a plague = what in the [expletive deleted]
2 grief/sorrow is
3 good faith ("I swear")★
4 cousin = relatives generally
5 objection
6 except, before excepted = object (as a lawyer does, in court), *exceptis
exceptiendis*, "with the exceptions previously noted"
7 (1) moderate, reasonable, (2) better★
8 confine myself no finer: Sir Toby is, as usual, distinctly tipsy; he perhaps
works away from "fine and dandy," meaning "excellent" but associating
"fine" (very good) with "dandy" (foppishly dressed), and derives his own
drunken meaning of "confine" as "clothe oneself"
9 if
10 bootstraps = loops sewed to the top of a boot, to aid in pulling it on
11 copious/deep drinking

15   brought in one night here to be her wooer.

Sir Toby   Who, Sir Andrew Aguecheek?[12]

Maria   Ay, he.

Sir Toby   He's as tall[13] a man as any's in Illyria.

Maria   What's that to th' purpose?

20   *Sir Toby*   Why, he has three thousand ducats[14] a year.

Maria   Ay, but he'll have but a year in all these ducats. He's a
         very fool and a prodigal.[15]

Sir Toby   Fie, that you'll say so. He plays o' the viol-de-
         gamboys,[16] and speaks three or four languages word for word
25   without book, and hath all the good gifts of nature.

Maria   He hath indeed, all most natural.[17] For besides that he's
         a fool, he's a great quarreler. And but that he hath the gift of a
         coward, to allay the gust[18] he hath in quarreling, 'tis thought
         among the prudent he would quickly have the gift of a grave.

30   *Sir Toby*   By this hand, they are scoundrels and subtractors[19] that
         say so of him. Who are they?

Maria   They that add, moreover, he's drunk nightly in your
         company.

Sir Toby   With drinking healths[20] to my niece. I'll drink to her as
35   long as there is a passage in my throat, and drink in Illyria.
         He's a coward and a coistrel[21] that will not drink to my niece

---

12 ague = fever, cheek = jaw, so "aguecheek" is something like "fever jaw" or
   "toothache" (EYGyouCHEEK)
13 (1) handsome, decent, (2) brave, courageous
14 gold coins
15 waster, spendthrift
16 viola da gamba, a predecessor of the cello
17 deficient in intelligence, fool-like
18 allay the gust = repress/subdue the liking/inclination/relish
19 detractors
20 toasts
21 knave, low/base fellow, stable hand (KOYstril)

till his brains turn[22] o' the toe like a parish-top.[23] What,
wench?[24] *Castiliano vulgo,* [25] for here comes Sir Andrew
Agueface.

ENTER SIR ANDREW AGUECHEEK

Sir Andrew	Sir Toby Belch. How now, Sir Toby Belch?	40
Sir Toby	Sweet[26] Sir Andrew.	
Sir Andrew	*(to Maria)* Bless you, fair shrew.[27]	
Maria	And you too, sir.	
Sir Toby	Accost,[28] Sir Andrew, accost.	
Sir Andrew	What's that?	45
Sir Toby	My niece's chambermaid.	
Sir Andrew	Good Mistress[29] Accost, I desire better acquaintance.	
Maria	My name is Mary, sir.	
Sir Andrew	Good Mistress Mary Accost –	
Sir Toby	You mistake, knight. "Accost" is front[30] her, board her, woo her, assail her.	50
Sir Andrew	By my troth, I would not undertake her[31] in this company. Is that the meaning of "accost"?	
Maria	Fare you well, gentlemen.	
Sir Toby	An thou let part so,[32] Sir Andrew, would thou mightst never draw sword again.	55

22 revolve, spin
23 large top for public use, spun by two people whipping it in opposite
   directions
24 woman, serving woman★
25 speak of the devil
26 delightful, pleasing, agreeable
27 scold (used generically for "woman")
28 go alongside, board, attack
29 Mrs. (used for women without regard to their marital status)
30 confront
31 undertake her = take her on, engage with her (sexual meaning)
32 let part so = allow her to leave in that way

Sir Andrew An you part so, mistress, I would I might never draw
sword again. Fair lady, do you think you have fools in hand?[33]

Maria   Sir, I have not you by th' hand.[34]

60 *Sir Andrew* Marry[35] but you shall have, and here's my hand.

Maria   Now, sir, "thought is free."[36] I pray you, bring your
hand to th' buttery-bar[37] and let it drink.

Sir Andrew Wherefore,[38] sweetheart? What's your metaphor?

Maria   It's dry,[39] sir.

65 *Sir Andrew* Why, I think so. I am not such an ass but I can keep
my hand dry. But what's your jest?

Maria   A dry jest, sir.

Sir Andrew Are you full of them?

Maria   Ay sir, I have them at my fingers' ends. Marry, now I
70 let go your hand, I am barren.[40]

EXIT MARIA

Sir Toby   O knight thou lackest a cup of canary.[41] When did I
see thee so put down?[42]

Sir Andrew Never in your life I think, unless you see canary put
me down. Methinks sometimes I have no more wit than a

33 in hand = here, in attendance
34 i.e., (1) she is not in direct attendance on/serving him; via Sir Toby, he is a
   guest in her mistress's house, and (2) he is a fool
35 an exclamation of surprise, indignation
36 unrestricted
37 buttery-bar = ledge on top of the buttery door, on which to set things
   (buttery = store room for food/liquor)
38 why
39 ironic (meaning her remark)
40 unproductive, dull (i.e., she can longer make dry jokes about fools, since she
   has broken contact with him)
41 wine (originally from the Canary Islands)
42 put down = crushed/humiliated/defeated/subdued★

Christian or an ordinary man has. But I am a great eater of   75
beef and I believe that does harm to my wit.

Sir Toby   No question.

Sir Andrew   An I thought that, I'ld forswear[43] it. I'll ride home
tomorrow, Sir Toby.

Sir Toby   *Pourquoi,* [44] my dear knight?   80

Sir Andrew   What is "pourquoi"? Do or not do? I would I had
bestowed[45] that time in the tongues[46] that I have in fencing,
dancing, and bear-baiting.[47] O had I but followed the arts![48]

Sir Toby   Then hadst thou had an excellent head of hair.

Sir Andrew   Why, would that have mended[49] my hair?   85

Sir Toby   Past question,[50] for thou seest it will not curl by
nature.

Sir Andrew   But it becomes me well enough, does't not?

Sir Toby   Excellent, it hangs like flax on a distaff,[51] and I hope
to see a housewife take thee between her legs and spin it off.   90

Sir Andrew   Faith, I'll home[52] tomorrow, Sir Toby. Your niece
will not[53] be seen, or if she be, it's four to one she'll[54] none of
me. The Count[55] himself here hard by[56] woos her.

---

43 renounce★
44 why (French)
45 applied, employed, given★
46 languages
47 popular entertainment, watching dogs attacking a bear chained to a stake★
48 followed the arts = pursued learning
49 improved
50 past question = without a doubt
51 in spinning, flax was wound on a cleft staff, a "distaff"
52 go home
53 will not = does not wish to
54 she'll = she wants
55 count = earl (the reference here is to the Duke)
56 hard by = near

Sir Toby   She'll none o' the count, she'll not match[57] above
95   her degree,[58] neither in estate, years, nor wit. I have heard her
swear't. Tut, there's life in't, man.

Sir Andrew I'll stay a month longer. I am a fellow o' the strangest
mind i' the world. I delight in masques and revels[59]
sometimes altogether.[60]

100 *Sir Toby*   Art thou good at these kickshawses,[61] knight?

Sir Andrew As any man in Illyria, whatsoever he be, under[62] the
degree of my betters, and yet I will not compare[63] with an
old man.

Sir Toby   What is thy excellence in a galliard,[64] knight?

105 *Sir Andrew* Faith, I can cut a caper.[65]

Sir Toby   And I can cut the mutton[66] to't.

Sir Andrew And I think I have the back-trick,[67] simply[68] as
strong as any man in Illyria.

Sir Toby   Wherefore are these things hid? Wherefore have
110   these gifts a curtain[69] before 'em? Are they like[70] to take[71]

57 marry
58 rank★
59 masques and revels = masquerade balls/dances and noisy merrymaking
60 totally, completely
61 trifling/frivolous affairs
62 below, lower than
63 be compared, likened
64 lively, fast-moving dance
65 cut a caper = dance friskily
66 caper, also meaning an herb used in pickling; it was often used on mutton
67 dancing backward
68 clearly
69 pictures hung on walls had protective curtains in front of them that were
    drawn back for viewing★
70 likely★
71 catch, accumulate, gather

dust, like Mistress Mall's[72] picture? Why dost thou not go to
church in a galliard, and come home in a coranto?[73] My very
walk should[74] be a jig, I would not so much as make water[75]
but in a sink-a-pace.[76] What dost thou mean?[77] Is it[78] a
world to hide virtues in? I did think, by the excellent   115
constitution[79] of thy leg, it was formed under the star[80] of a
galliard.

Sir Andrew Ay, 'tis strong, and it does indifferent[81] well in a
damned-colored[82] stock.[83] Shall we set about some revels?

Sir Toby What shall we do else? Were we not born under   120
Taurus?[84]

Sir Andrew Taurus? That's sides and heart.

Sir Toby No sir, it is legs and thighs. Let me see the caper. Ha,
higher. Ha, ha, excellent!

EXEUNT

72 Molly/Mary, i.e., the Virgin Mary, whose portrait, at that time, would have
   been taken down and hidden, as a dangerous symbol of Catholicism
73 coranto = courant, a running/gliding dance
74 would (i.e., were I you)
75 so much as make water = even urinate
76 sink-a-pace = cinquepace, a lively dance, very like the galliard
77 i.e., what are you up to/intending?
78 this
79 physical state
80 astrological influence/direction/destiny (i.e., "a dancing star")
81 fairly, equally
82 (?) damnably colored = highly/superlatively colored
83 stocking? tight boots?
84 astrological sign of the bull

SCENE 4

Duke Orsino's palace

ENTER VALENTINE AND VIOLA IN MAN'S ATTIRE

Valentine If the Duke continue these favors[1] towards you,
    Cesario, you are like to be much advanced. He hath known
    you but three days, and already you are no stranger.

Viola   You either fear his humor,[2] or my negligence, that you
5   call in question the continuance of his love.[3] Is he inconstant,
    sir, in his favors?

Valentine No, believe me.

Viola   I thank you. Here comes the Count.

ENTER ORSINO, CURIO, AND ATTENDANTS

Orsino   Who saw Cesario, ho?
10 *Viola*   On your attendance,[4] my lord: here.
Orsino   Stand you a while aloof,[5] Cesario,
    Thou know'st no less but all. I have unclasped[6]
    To thee the book even of my secret soul.
    Therefore good youth, address thy gait[7] unto her,
15   Be not denied access,[8] stand at her doors,
    And tell them, there thy fixèd[9] foot shall grow
    Till thou have audience.[10]

1 preference, liking
2 disposition ("moods")
3 kindness, regard
4 on your attendance = at your service
5 stand . . . aloof = stay there
6 opened
7 address thy gait = direct your walk★
8 be NOT denIED acCESS stand AT her DOORS
9 firm, attached
10 a hearing

Viola   Sure, my noble lord,

   If she be so abandoned to her sorrow

   As it is spoke, she never will admit me.

Orsino Be clamorous[11] and leap all civil bounds[12]   20

   Rather than make unprofited[13] return.

Viola   Say I do speak with her, my lord, what then?

Orsino O then, unfold[14] the passion of my love,

   Surprise[15] her with discourse of my dear faith.[16]

   It shall become thee well to act my woes.   25

   She will attend[17] it better in thy youth

   Than in a nuncio's[18] of more grave aspect.[19]

Viola   I think not so, my lord.

Orsino   Dear lad, believe it,

   For they shall yet belie[20] thy happy years,

   That[21] say thou art a man. Diana's[22] lip   30

   Is not more smooth and rubious.[23] Thy small pipe[24]

   Is as the maiden's organ, shrill and sound,[25]

   And all is semblative[26] a woman's part.[27]

---

11 noisy
12 civil bounds = limits of good manners / civility
13 useless, empty
14 spread out, disclose, explain
15 overpower, ambush
16 dear faith = worthy / honorable faithfulness
17 listen to
18 messenger, representative
19 grave aspect = serious / weighty / solemn appearance / look
20 misrepresent, give false account of
21 those who
22 goddess of moon / hunting, protectress of women
23 ruby-colored
24 voice
25 shrill and sound = high-pitched and unspoiled
26 resembling
27 allotted portion, function, character

I know thy constellation[28] is right apt[29]

35   For this affair.[30] Some four or five attend him –
All,[31] if you will, for I myself am best
When least in company. Prosper well in this,
And thou shalt live as freely[32] as thy lord,
To[33] call his fortunes thine.

40   *Viola* I'll do my best
To woo your lady. (*aside*) Yet, a barful strife,[34]
Whoe'er I woo, myself would[35] be his wife.

EXEUNT

28 character, disposition (as dictated by astrological imperatives)
29 right apt = completely suited/fitted/prepared★
30 business★
31 all of you (attendants)
32 without limitation, liberally, nobly
33 and
34 barful strife = difficult/challenging struggle/conflict
35 wish to

SCENE 5

Olivia's house

ENTER MARIA AND FESTE,[1] A CLOWN

Maria Nay, either tell me where thou hast been, or I will not
open my lips so wide as a bristle[2] may enter, in way of thy
excuse. My lady will hang thee for thy absence.

Feste Let her hang me. He that is well hanged in this world[3]
needs to fear no colors.[4]   5

Maria Make that good.[5]

Feste He shall see none to fear.

Maria A good Lenten[6] answer. I can tell thee where that saying
was born, of "I fear no colors."[7]

Feste Where, good Mistress Mary?   10

Maria In the wars, and that may you be bold[8] to say in your
foolery.

Feste Well, God give them wisdom that have it. And those that
are fools, let them use their talents.

Maria Yet you will be hanged for being so long absent, or to be   15
turned away.[9] Is not that as good as a hanging to you?

Feste Many a good hanging prevents a bad marriage. And for[10]

1 FEstay (from French *fête* – Old French *feste*, Latin *festus*, "festive, joyous")
2 stiff hair
3 the virtues of a man being "well hung" – having large genitals – were
  recognized in Shakespeare's time (see *OED, hung*, 2b)
4 (1) enemies, (2) those who wear collars ("authority") or those who have the
  "colors/appearances" of authority, (3) the hangman's noose
5 valid, adequate ("prove it")
6 meager, dismal
7 enemy ("military insignia, flags, etc.")
8 courageous, daring, brave
9 turned away = dismissed, discharged
10 as for

turning away, let summer bear it out.[11]

Maria   You are resolute,[12] then?

20   *Feste*   Not so neither, but I am resolved on two points.[13]

Maria   That if one break, the other will hold. Or if both break, your gaskins[14] fall.

Feste   Apt, in good faith, very apt. Well, go thy way. If Sir Toby would leave drinking,[15] thou wert as witty a piece of Eve's

25   flesh as any in Illyria.

Maria   Peace[16] you rogue,[17] no more o' that. Here comes my lady. Make your excuse wisely, you were best.[18]

EXIT MARIA

Feste   Wit, an't be thy will, put me into good fooling! Those wits[19] that think they have thee,[20] do very oft prove fools.

30   And I that am sure I lack thee, may pass for a wise man. For what says Quinapalus?[21] "Better a witty fool, than a foolish wit."

ENTER OLIVIA WITH MALVOLIO[22]

God bless thee, lady!

Olivia   Take the fool away.

11 bear it out = demonstrate / testify to it
12 determined, positive
13 "point" also means "garter"
14 hose
15 i.e., a condition that is impossible ("never")
16 be quiet*
17 rascal
18 you were best = you'd better
19 clever / talented / witty people
20 wit ("brains")
21 an invented name / person
22 from Italian: ill-willed, malevolent (malVOHLyo)

Feste Do you not hear, fellows?[23] Take away the lady.

Olivia Go to,[24] you're a dry[25] fool. I'll no more of you. Besides,   35
you grow dishonest.[26]

Feste Two faults, madonna,[27] that drink and good counsel will
amend.[28] For give the dry fool drink, then is the fool not dry.
Bid the dishonest man mend himself – if he mend, he is no
longer dishonest. If he cannot, let the botcher[29] mend him.   40
Anything that's mended is but patched.[30] Virtue that
transgresses[31] is but patched with sin, and sin that amends is
but patched with virtue. If that[32] this simple syllogism will
serve,[33] so. If it will not, what remedy?[34] As there is no true
cuckold but calamity,[35] so[36] beauty's a flower. The lady   45
bade[37] "take away the fool." Therefore, I say again, take her
away.

Olivia Sir, I bade them take away *you*.

Feste Misprision[38] in the highest degree![39] Lady, *cucullus non*

23 comrades
24 come on★
25 sterile, barren
26 deceitful, dishonorable, unreliable
27 my lady
28 correct, reform★
29 repairman
30 i.e., like his traditional fool's costume
31 sins
32 then
33 be worthy, do the job
34 cure
35 (?) men are married to fortune, so bad fortune makes a man a cuckold
36 so too
37 ordered
38 mistake, offense
39 extent, stage

50   *facit monachum.*[40] That's as much to say as I wear not motley[41]
     in my brain. Good madonna, give me leave[42] to prove you a
     fool.

     Olivia   Can you do it?

     Feste   Dexteriously,[43] good madonna.

55   Olivia   Make your proof.

     Feste   I must catechize you for it, madonna. Good my
     mouse[44] of virtue, answer me.

     Olivia   Well, sir, for want[45] of other idleness,[46] I'll bide[47] your
     proof.

60   Feste   Good madonna, why mournest thou?

     Olivia   Good fool, for my brother's death.

     Feste   I think his soul is in hell, madonna.

     Olivia   I know his soul is in heaven, fool.

     Feste   The more fool, madonna, to mourn for your brother's
65   soul being in heaven. Take away the fool, gentlemen.

     Olivia   What think you of this fool, Malvolio? Doth he not
     mend?

     Malvolio Yes, and shall do till the pangs of death shake him.
     Infirmity,[48] that decays the wise, doth ever make the better
70   fool.

     Feste   God send you, sir, a speedy infirmity, for the better
     increasing your folly. Sir Toby will be sworn that I am no

40 wearing a monk's cowl does not make you a monk
41 a fool's multi-colored costume
42 permission★
43 nimbly, skillfully, cleverly ("dexterously")
44 dear lady (mouse = term of endearment, used for women)
45 lack
46 inactivity, foolishness, triviality
47 submit to, wait for
48 (1) weakness, inability, (2) sickness, (3) old age

fox,[49] but he will not pass[50] his word for two pence[51] that
you are no fool.

Olivia   How say you to that, Malvolio?   75

Malvolio I marvel your ladyship takes delight in such a barren
rascal. I saw him put down the other day with[52] an ordinary
fool that has no more brain than a stone. Look you now, he's
out of his guard[53] already. Unless you laugh and minister
occasion to him, he is gagged. I protest,[54] I take these wise   80
men, that crow so at these set[55] kind of fools, no better than
the fools' zanies.[56]

Olivia   Oh, you are sick of[57] self-love, Malvolio, and taste with
a distempered[58] appetite. To be generous,[59] guiltless, and of
free disposition,[60] is[61] to take those things for bird-bolts[62]   85
that you deem cannon-bullets. There is no slander in an
allowed[63] fool, though he do nothing but rail,[64] nor no
railing in a known discreet man, though he do nothing but
reprove.[65]

49 i.e., clever, cunning
50 speak
51 TUPens
52 by
53 out of his guard = has no defenses left
54 declare, affirm★
55 deliberate, intentional
56 a comic/clown who mimics other comics/clowns as they perform
57 with
58 vexed, troubled, out of humor
59 high-spirited
60 (1) position, condition, plans, (2) bestowal, control★
61 means
62 blunted arrows used for shooting birds
63 licensed
64 scold
65 scold, censure★

90   *Feste* Now Mercury endue thee with leasing,[66] for thou
      speakest well of fools.

ENTER MARIA

    Maria Madam, there is at the gate a young gentleman much[67]
      desires to speak with you.

    Olivia From the Count Orsino, is it?

95   *Maria* I know not, madam. 'Tis a fair young man, and well
      attended.[68]

    Olivia Who of my people hold[69] him in delay?[70]

    Maria Sir Toby, madam, your kinsman.

    Olivia Fetch him off,[71] I pray you, he speaks nothing but

100   madman.[72] Fie on him!

EXIT MARIA

    Go you, Malvolio. If it be a suit from the count, I am sick, or
    not at home. What you will, to dismiss it.[73]

EXIT MALVOLIO

    (*to Feste*) Now you see, sir, how your fooling grows old, and
    people dislike it.

105 *Feste* Thou hast spoke for us,[74] madonna, as if thy eldest son

---

66 endue thee with leasing = instruct you in lying/deception (Mercury: god of
    trickery and lying)
67 who much
68 served, accompanied
69 are keeping
70 in delay = waiting
71 fetch him off = remove Sir Toby
72 lunacy, foolishness
73 what you will, to dismiss it = do whatever you like to send this person away
74 i.e., we fools

should be[75] a fool. (*seeing Sir Toby*) Whose skull Jove[76] cram
with brains, for here he comes. One of thy kin has a most
weak pia mater.[77]

ENTER SIR TOBY

Olivia   By mine honor,[78] half drunk. What is he at the gate,
cousin?[79]   110
Sir Toby   A gentleman.
Olivia   A gentleman? What gentleman?
Sir Toby   'Tis a gentleman here.[80] (*he belches*) A plague o' these
pickle-herring! (*to Feste*) How now, sot![81]
Feste   Good Sir Toby.   115
Olivia   Cousin, cousin, how have you come so early by this
lethargy?[82]
Sir Toby   Lechery! I defy[83] lechery. There's one[84] at the gate.
Olivia   Ay, marry, what is he?
Sir Toby   Let him be the devil, an he will, I care not. Give me   120
faith, say I. Well, it's all one.

EXIT SIR TOBY

Olivia   What's a drunken man like, fool?
Feste   Like a drowned man, a fool, and a mad man. One

75 should be = were
76 may Jove
77 pia mater = brain
78 by mine honor = by my word
79 a generic term for any relative, not confined to "cousin"
80 'tis a gentleman here = there is a gentleman who has come here
81 fool★
82 apathy, inertia
83 repudiate, challenge★
84 someone

draught above heat[85] makes him a fool, the second mads him,

125   and a third drowns him.

Olivia   Go thou and seek the crowner,[86] and let him sit[87] o'

my coz, for he's in the third degree of drink, he's drowned.

Go look after him.

Feste   He is but mad yet, madonna, and the fool shall look

130   to[88] the madman.

EXIT FESTE

ENTER MALVOLIO

Malvolio   Madam, yond young fellow[89] swears he will speak with

you. I told him you were sick, he takes on him[90] to

understand so much, and therefore comes to speak with you.

I told him you were asleep, he seems to have a foreknowledge

135   of that too, and therefore comes to speak with you. What is to

be said to him, lady? He's fortified[91] against any denial.

Olivia   Tell him he shall not speak with me.

Malvolio   H'as[92] been told so. And he says he'll stand at your

door like a sheriff's post,[93] and be the supporter[94] to a bench,

140   but he'll speak with you.

85 draught above heat = drink (DRAFT) beyond/more than alcohol's
warming effect

86 coroner

87 hold a hearing/inquest

88 look to = attend to, take care of★

89 man (often used condescendingly of someone of clearly lower rank than
oneself)★

90 takes on him = undertakes, assumes, pretends

91 protected

92 ha's = ha' has, he has

93 sheriff's posts = two painted posts at a sheriff's door, to which
proclamations were nailed

94 prop, bench post

Olivia   What kind o' man is he?

Malvolio Why, of mankind.

Olivia   What manner[95] of man?

Malvolio Of very ill manner. He'll speak with you, will you
or no.   145

Olivia   Of what personage[96] and years is he?

Malvolio Not yet old enough for a man, nor young enough for a
boy, as a squash[97] is before 'tis a peascod,[98] or a codling[99]
when 'tis almost an apple. 'Tis with him in standing[100] water,
between boy and man. He is very well-favored[101] and he   150
speaks very shrewishly.[102] One would think his mother's milk
were scarce out of him.

Olivia   Let him approach. Call in my gentlewoman.

Malvolio Gentlewoman, my lady calls.

EXIT MALVOLIO

ENTER MARIA

Olivia   Give me my veil. Come, throw it o'er my face.   155
We'll once more hear Orsino's embassy.[103]

ENTER VIOLA, DISGUISED AS CESARIO, AND ATTENDANTS

Viola   The honorable lady of the house, which is she?

---

95 nature, sort
96 appearance
97 unripe pea pod
98 pea pod
99 immature / half-ripe apple
100 stagnant
101 good-looking, handsome
102 ill-tempered, tart
103 ambassador

Olivia Speak to me, I shall answer[104] for her. Your will?

Viola Most radiant, exquisite, and unmatchable beauty – I pray
you, tell me if this be the lady of the house, for I never saw[105]
her. I would be loath to cast[106] away my speech, for besides
that it is excellently well penned, I have taken great pains to
con[107] it. Good beauties, let me sustain[108] no scorn, I am very
comptible,[109] even to the least sinister usage.[110]

Olivia Whence came you, sir?

Viola I can say little more than I have studied,[111] and that
question's out of[112] my part.[113] Good gentle[114] one, give me
modest assurance[115] if you be the lady of the house, that I
may proceed in my speech.

Olivia Are you a comedian?[116]

Viola No, my profound heart.[117] And yet (by the very fangs of
malice[118] I swear) I am not that I play.[119] Are you the lady of
the house?

Olivia If I do not usurp[120] myself, I am.

104 (1) respond, (2) be responsible★
105 have seen
106 throw★
107 memorize★
108 endure
109 sensitive
110 sinister usage = unfavorable/adverse treatment
111 learned, memorized
112 out of = beyond, outside
113 role
114 well-born, noble★
115 promise, guarantee★
116 (1) actor, (2) comic actor
117 (1) (*of Olivia*) my wise/knowing dear/lady, *or* (2) (*of herself*) by my
knowing heart
118 fangs of malice = teeth of ill-will
119 that I play = what I am portraying/representing
120 (1) intrude, encroach upon, (2) unlawfully seize/appropriate, (3) supplant★

Viola Most certain, if you are she, you do usurp yourself, for   175
what is yours to bestow is not yours to reserve.[121] But this is
from[122] my commission.[123] I will on with my speech in your
praise, and then show you the heart of my message.

Olivia Come to what is important in't. I forgive[124] you the
praise.   180

Viola Alas, I took great pains to study it, and 'tis poetical.

Olivia It is the more like to be feigned,[125] I pray you keep it in.
I heard you were saucy[126] at my gates, and allowed[127] your
approach rather to wonder[128] at you than to hear you. If you
be not mad, be gone. If you have reason,[129] be brief. 'Tis not   185
that time of moon with me[130] to make one[131] in so
skipping[132] a dialogue.

Maria Will you hoist sail, sir? Here lies your way.[133]

Viola No, good swabber,[134] I am to hull[135] here a little longer.
Some mollification[136] for your giant,[137] sweet lady. Tell me   190

121 refrain from giving (a veiled reference to her refusal to marry Orsino)
122 outside
123 instructions
124 excuse
125 contrived, pretended
126 rude, cheeky, presumptuous★
127 I allowed
128 marvel
129 something to say
130 'tis not that time of moon with me = (1) I am not lunatic enough, (2) I am
     not in the mood, (3) it is not the right time in my menstrual cycle
131 make one = to participate ("to be someone")
132 hopping, jumping, trivial
133 path, road★
134 sailor (negative tone)
135 float
136 softening, pacification
137 (1) protective monster / watchman, *or* (2) an ironic reference to Maria's
     small size

your mind,[138] I am a messenger.[139]

Olivia Sure, you have some hideous matter[140] to deliver,[141] when the courtesy of it is so fearful.[142] Speak your office.[143]

Viola It alone[144] concerns your ear. I bring no overture[145] of

195 war, no taxation[146] of homage,[147] I hold the olive[148] in my hand, my words are as full of peace as matter.

Olivia Yet you began rudely.[149] What are you? What would[150] you?

Viola The rudeness that hath appeared in me have I learned

200 from my entertainment.[151] What I am, and what I would, are as secret as maidenhead.[152] To your ears, divinity.[153] To any other's, profanation.[154]

Olivia (*to her servants*) Give us the place alone, we will hear this divinity.

EXEUNT MARIA AND ATTENDANTS

205 Now, sir, what is your text?[155]

Viola Most sweet lady –

138 your mind = what you really think
139 i.e., I will transmit what you have to say
140 subject, material★
141 speak, express★
142 terrible, dreadful
143 business
144 only
145 disclosure, declaration
146 imposition
147 reverence, acknowledgment (of beauty)
148 olive branch (of peace)
149 violently★
150 want, wish
151 treatment, reception★
152 virginity
153 divine virtue, holy message
154 desecration/pollution of the sacred
155 theme, subject

Olivia A comfortable[156] doctrine, and much may be said of it.
Where lies your text?

Viola In Orsino's bosom.[157]

Olivia In his bosom? In what chapter[158] of his bosom?   210

Viola To answer by the method,[159] in the first[160] of his heart.

Olivia O, I have read it. It is heresy.[161] Have you no more to say?

Viola Good madam, let me see your face.

Olivia Have you any commission from your lord to negotiate
with[162] my face? You are now out of[163] your text. But we   215
will draw the curtain and show you the picture. (*she unveils*)
Look you, sir, such a one I was this present.[164] Is't not well
done?

Viola Excellently done, if God did all.[165]

Olivia 'Tis in grain[166] sir, 'twill endure wind and weather.   220

Viola 'Tis beauty truly blent,[167] whose red and white
Nature's own sweet and cunning[168] hand laid on.
Lady, you are the cruell'st she alive,
If you will lead these graces[169] to the grave,
And leave the world no copy.   225

Olivia O sir, I will not be so hard-hearted. I will give out divers

156 reassuring, inspiring
157 breast
158 section, part
159 same procedure (i.e., biblical style)
160 foremost ("preceding all others")
161 heretical (i.e., not valid)
162 about
163 out of = departed/strayed from
164 this present = as of right now★ (portrait paintings were usually dated)
165 (i.e., if there has been no cosmetic improvement)
166 in grain = natural, genuine
167 blended
168 skillful, expert, clever★
169 charms, elegances★

schedules[170] of my beauty. It shall be inventoried[171] and
every particle and utensil[172] labeled to my will.[173] As, item,
two lips, indifferent[174] red; item, two gray eyes, with lids to
230　them; item, one neck, one chin, and so forth. Were you sent
hither to praise me?

Viola　I see you what you are, you are too proud.

But if you were the devil, you are fair.

My lord and master loves you. O such love

235　Could be but recompensed,[175] though you were crowned

The nonpareil[176] of beauty.

Olivia　　　　　　　　　　　　How does he love me?

Viola　With adorations, fertile[177] tears,

With groans that thunder love, with sighs of fire.[178]

Olivia　Your lord does know[179] my mind, I cannot love him.

240　Yet I suppose him virtuous, know him noble,

Of great estate, of fresh and stainless youth,

In voices[180] well divulged,[181] free,[182] learn'd, and valiant,[183]

170　divers schedules = numerous/assorted lists ("writings") (SHEDyules)
171　cataloged
172　particle and utensil = part/portion and implement/instrument (i.e., as in an ordinary inventory)
173　labeled [verb] to my will = affixed as an explanatory appendix to my last will and testament
174　more or less ("neutral")
175　could be but recompensed = should only be rewarded*
176　matchless/peerless one
177　abundant, prolific
178　great heat/warmth
179　does know = knows (do: often an intensifier of the verb that follows it rather than an independent verb)
180　general opinion
181　proclaimed, declared
182　generous, magnanimous
183　(1) stalwart, strong, (2) bold, courageous (inVOIcesWELL diVULGED free LEARND andVALyent)

And in dimension[184] and the shape of nature
A gracious[185] person, but yet I cannot love him.   245
He might have took his answer long ago.

Viola If I did love you in my master's flame,
With such a suffering, such a deadly life,[186]
In your denial I would find no sense,
I would not understand it.

Olivia   Why, what would you?

Viola Make me a willow[187] cabin at your gate,   250
And call upon my soul[188] within the house,
Write loyal cantons[189] of contemnèd[190] love,
And sing them loud even in the dead of night.
Halloo your name to the reverberate[191] hills
And make the babbling gossip of the air[192]   255
Cry out "Olivia!" O you should not rest
Between the elements of air and earth,
But you should pity me.

Olivia   You might do much.[193]
What is your parentage?

Viola Above my fortunes, yet my state[194] is well.   260
I am a gentleman.

Olivia   Get you to your lord.

---

184 proportions
185 pleasing
186 spirit, vigor, intensity
187 willow: symbol of unrequited love
188 i.e., Olivia (he has given her his soul/heart; they are now located in her)
189 loyal cantons = faithful songs
190 despised
191 (adjective) reverberating, echoing
192 the babbling gossip of the air: Echo, the chattering nymph
193 do much = go far
194 circumstances★

I cannot love him. Let him send no more,

Unless (perchance) you come to me again,

To tell me how he takes it. Fare you well.

265   I thank you for your pains.[195] (*offers money*) Spend this for
me.

Viola   I am no fee'd post,[196] lady, keep your purse.

My master, not myself, lacks recompense.

Love[197] make his heart of flint, that[198] you shall[199] love,

And let your fervor[200] like my master's be,[201]

270   Placed in contempt. Farewell, fair cruelty.

EXIT VIOLA

Olivia   "What is your parentage?"

"Above my fortunes, yet my state is well.

I am a gentleman." I'll be sworn thou art,

Thy tongue, thy face, thy limbs, actions, and spirit,[202]

275   Do give thee five-fold blazon.[203] Not too fast. Soft,[204] soft,

Unless[205] the master were the man.[206] How now?

Even so quickly may one catch the plague?[207]

Methinks I feel this youth's perfections

195 troubles
196 fee'd (adjective) post = hired/paid messenger
197 may love
198 he who
199 will
200 passion ("heat")
201 is
202 thy TONGUE thy FACE thy LIMBS acTIONS and SPIrit
203 markings on a heraldic coat of arms, indicative of degrees of gentility
204 be calm
205 except if
206 were the man = Viola were the Duke and not the Duke's servant
207 i.e., the illness of love

With an invisible and subtle stealth[208]
To creep in at mine eyes.[209] Well, let it be.   280
What ho, Malvolio!

ENTER MALVOLIO

Malvolio   Here madam, at your service.
Olivia   Run after that same peevish[210] messenger,
    The County's[211] man. He left this ring behind him,
    Would I or not.[212] Tell him I'll none of it.
    Desire him not to flatter with[213] his lord,   285
    Nor hold him up[214] with hopes. I am not for him.
    If that the youth will come this way tomorrow,
    I'll give him reasons for't. Hie[215] thee, Malvolio.
Malvolio Madam, I will.

EXIT MALVOLIO

Olivia   I do I know not what, and fear to find   290
    Mine eye too great a flatterer for my mind.[216]
    Fate, show thy force,[217] ourselves we do not owe.[218]
    What is decreed must be, and be this so.

EXIT

208 subtle stealth = penetrating/elusive/delicate thievery
209 as in *Romeo and Juliet*, love was thought to enter through the eyes and be
    thereby communicated directly to the heart
210 foolish, irritable, stubborn★
211 Count's
212 whether I wanted it or not
213 flatter with = flatter ("with" = "to"; modern English dispenses with the
    preposition)
214 hold him up = preserve, maintain
215 hurry
216 i.e., that my sight praises falsely to, and thus deceives, my mind
217 strength, power
218 own, possess

Act 2

❦

The seacoast

ENTER ANTONIO AND SEBASTIAN

Antonio   Will you stay no longer? Nor will you not that I go
with you?

Sebastian By your patience,[1] no. My stars shine darkly over me,
the malignancy[2] of my fate might perhaps distemper[3] yours.

5   Therefore I shall crave[4] of you your leave, that[5] I may bear my
evils[6] alone. It were a bad recompense for your love, to lay
any of them on you.

Antonio   Let me yet know of you[7] whither you are bound.

Sebastian No sooth,[8] sir. My determinate[9] voyage is mere

---

1 by your patience = with your permission, pardon me
2 malevolence
3 impair, dilute, disturb
4 ask★
5 so that
6 calamities, misfortunes
7 let me yet know of you = still, tell me
8 truly, in truth★
9 planned, intended

extravagancy.[10] But I perceive in you so excellent a touch of   10
modesty,[11] that you will not extort[12] from me what I am
willing[13] to keep in. Therefore it charges[14] me in manners[15]
the rather[16] to express[17] myself. You must know of me then,
Antonio, my name is Sebastian (which I called[18] Rodorigo).
My father was that Sebastian of Messaline, whom I know you   15
have heard of. He left behind him myself and a sister, both
born in an hour.[19] If the heavens had been pleased, would we
had so ended! But you, sir, altered that, for some hour[20]
before you took me from the breach[21] of the sea was my
sister drowned.   20

Antonio   Alas the day!

Sebastian   A lady, sir, though it was said she much resembled me,
was yet of[22] many accounted[23] beautiful. But though I could
not with such estimable wonder[24] overfar[25] believe that, yet
thus far I will boldly publish[26] her, she bore a mind that   25
envy[27] could not but call fair. She is drowned already, sir, with

10 mere extravagancy = pure vagrancy/wandering
11 touch of modesty = sense of self-control/moderation
12 wring, wrest
13 desiring, wanting
14 obliges
15 good manners
16 the rather = all the sooner
17 show, reveal, speak of
18 which I called = though I gave myself the name of
19 in an hour = within an hour of each other
20 for some hour = because roughly/approximately an hour
21 breaking waves
22 by
23 considered
24 estimable wonder = high degree of admiration
25 fully
26 publicly declare
27 ill-will, malice★

salt water, though I seem to drown her remembrance again with more.[28]

Antonio   Pardon me, sir, your bad entertainment.

30   *Sebastian*   O good Antonio, forgive me your trouble.[29]

Antonio   If you will[30] not murder me for my love,[31] let me be your servant.

Sebastian   If you will not undo what you have done, that is, kill him whom you have recovered,[32] desire it not. Fare ye well at

35   once. My bosom is full of kindness,[33] and I am yet so near[34] the manners of my mother, that upon the least[35] occasion more mine eyes will tell tales of me.[36] I am bound to the Count Orsino's court. Farewell.

EXIT SEBASTIAN

Antonio   The gentleness[37] of all the gods go with thee!

40   I have many enemies in Orsino's court,
Else would I very shortly see thee there.
But come what may, I do adore[38] thee so,
That danger shall[39] seem sport,[40] and I will go.

EXIT

28 i.e., he is weeping
29 i.e., the trouble/pains that Sebastian has caused Antonio
30 wish, want
31 for my love = by leaving me, knowing my regard for you
32 reclaimed/rescued from the sea
33 affection
34 like
35 slightest
36 i.e., he will weep
37 kindness
38 respect, like
39 must
40 amusement, entertainment

SCENE 2
A street

Malvolio Were not you even[1] now with the Countess Olivia?

Viola Even now sir, on a moderate pace, I have since arrived
but hither.[2]

Malvolio She returns this ring to you, sir. You might have saved
me my pains, to have[3] taken it away yourself. She adds, 5
moreover, that you should put your lord into a desperate[4]
assurance she will none of him. And one thing more, that you
be never so hardy to[5] come again in his affairs, unless it be to
report your lord's taking of this. Receive it so.[6]

Viola She took the ring of me, I'll[7] none of it. 10

Malvolio Come sir, you peevishly threw it to her. And her will
is, it should be so returned. (*throws it on the ground*) If it be
worth stooping for, there it lies in your eye.[8] If not, be it his
that finds it.

Viola I left no ring with her. What means this lady? 15
Fortune forbid[9] my outside[10] have not charmed[11] her!

1 just
2 but hither = only to here
3 to have = if you had
4 hopeless★
5 hardy to = daring/bold as to
6 accordingly, thus
7 I'll = I want
8 sight
9 fortune forbid = chance/luck★ prohibit, prevent
10 appearance (deceptive, since she is wearing male clothing)
11 bewitched, enchanted

She made good view[12] of me, indeed so much,
That sure methought her eyes had lost[13] her tongue,
For she did speak in starts distractedly.[14]
20 She loves me sure,[15] the cunning of her passion
Invites[16] me in[17] this churlish[18] messenger.
(*examines ring*) None of my lord's ring![19] Why, he sent her
none.
I am the man.[20] If it be so, as 'tis,
Poor lady, she were better[21] love a dream.
25 Disguise, I see thou art a wickedness,
Wherein the pregnant enemy[22] does much.
How easy is it,[23] for the proper false[24]
In women's waxen[25] hearts to set their forms.[26]
Alas, our frailty is the cause, not we,
30 For such as we are made of, such we be.
How will this fadge?[27] My master loves her dearly,
And I (poor monster) fond[28] as much on him.

12 inspection, examination, survey ("seeing")
13 deprived her of
14 starts distractedly = leaps/spurts/jumps disjointedly/agitated
15 certainly
16 encourages
17 through, by means of
18 boorish, surly, rude
19 rings
20 (i.e., she chooses me, not the Duke)
21 were better = would do better to
22 pregnant enemy = fertile/inventive/resourceful* devil
23 is it = it is
24 proper false = inherent deceit
25 wax-like, soft and impressible/impressionable/susceptible
26 set their forms = fix/arrange the shapes of their hearts
27 work out, go on, make its way
28 infatuated

And she (mistaken) seems to dote on[29] me.
What will become of this? As I am man,[30]
My state is desperate for my master's love.   35
As I am woman (now alas the day!)
What thriftless[31] sighs shall poor Olivia breathe?
O time, thou must untangle this, not I,
It is too hard a knot for me t'untie.[32]

EXIT VIOLA

29 dote on = to be infatuated with
30 as I am man = to the extent that I am/look like a man
31 unfortunate, useless, wasteful
32 to untie

SCENE 3

Olivia's house

ENTER SIR TOBY BELCH AND SIR ANDREW

Sir Toby   Approach, Sir Andrew. Not to be abed after
midnight is to be up betimes,[1] and *deliculo surgere,* [2] thou
know'st.

Sir Andrew Nay my troth I know not. But I know, to be up late
is to be up late.

Sir Toby   A false conclusion. I hate it as[3] an unfilled can.[4] To
be up after midnight and to go to bed then, is early. So that to
go to bed after midnight is to go to bed betimes. Does not
our life consist of the four elements?[5]

Sir Andrew Faith, so they say, but I think it rather consists of
eating and drinking.

Sir Toby   Thou'rt a scholar, let us therefore eat and drink.
Marian, I say! a stoup[6] of wine!

ENTER FESTE

Sir Andrew Here comes the fool, i' faith.

Feste   How now, my hearts.[7] Did you never see the picture
of We Three?[8]

Sir Toby   Welcome, ass. Now let's have a catch.[9]

1 early
2 early rising is good for the health
3 just as I hate
4 container for liquids
5 earth, water, air, fire
6 container, tankard
7 companions
8 two donkeys; the viewer/spectator is the third
9 song (i.e., sing for us, as fools were expected to do)

Sir Andrew By my troth, the fool has an excellent breast.[10] I had
rather than forty shillings[11] I had such a leg, and so sweet a
breath to sing, as the fool has. In sooth, thou wast in very   20
gracious fooling last night, when thou spokest of
Pigrogromitus, of the Vapians passing the equinoctial of
Queubus.[12] 'Twas very good, i' faith. I sent thee sixpence[13]
for thy leman.[14] Hadst it?[15]

Feste   I did impeticos thy gratillity,[16] for Malvolio's nose is   25
no whipstock,[17] my lady has a white hand, and the
Myrmidons[18] are no bottle-ale[19] houses.

Sir Andrew Excellent! Why, this is the best fooling, when all is
done. Now, a song.

Sir Toby   Come on, there is sixpence for you. Let's have   30
a song.

Sir Andrew There's a testril[20] of me too. If one knight give a – [21]

Feste   Would you have a love song, or a song of good life?[22]

Sir Toby   A love song, a love song.

Sir Andrew Ay, ay. I care not for good life.   35

Feste   (*sings*)

10 chest, lungs, singing voice
11 40 shillings = 2 British pounds
12 nonsense words
13 12 pence = 1 shilling
14 sweetheart
15 hadst it = did you get it
16 impetitcos thy gratillity = pocket your tip
17 whip-handle
18 Thessalians who fought at Troy, under Achilles
19 beer
20 sixpence
21 (?) unexplained; perhaps a printer's error
22 (?) the "good life" as in "good cheer" (i.e., as in a drinking toast)? Or "good
life" as in a moral/virtuous life?

O mistress mine, where are you roaming?

O stay and hear,[23] your true love's coming,

    That can sing both high and low.

40   Trip no further, pretty sweeting.

Journeys end in lovers meeting,

    Every wise man's son[24] doth know.

Sir Andrew Excellent good, i' faith.

Sir Toby   Good, good.

45 *Feste*   (*sings*)

What is love? 'Tis not hereafter,

Present mirth hath present laughter,

    What's to come is still unsure.

In delay there lies no plenty,

50   Then come kiss me, sweet and twenty.

    Youth's a stuff[25] will not endure.

Sir Andrew A mellifluous voice, as I am true[26] knight.

Sir Toby   A contagious breath.[27]

Sir Andrew Very sweet and contagious, i' faith.

55 *Sir Toby*   To hear by the nose, it is dulcet in contagion.[28] But shall we make the welkin dance[29] indeed? Shall we rouse the night-owl[30] in a catch[31] that will draw three souls out of one

---

23 stay and hear = stop and listen

24 "wise men have foolish children" (proverb)

25 stock, supplies, stores ("material")

26 a true

27 contagious breath = catchy sound? Or, if Sir Toby is laying a trap for Sir Andrew, an infectious sound?

28 dulcet in contagion = sweet in its infectiousness (ironic)

29 welkin dance = sky/heavens★ leap

30 rouse the night-owl = wake up the now-sleeping owl that has been flying all night

31 round (sung by two or more people, each starting at the same interval after the person before)

weaver?[32] Shall we do that?

Sir Andrew An you love me, let's do't. I am dog[33] at a catch.

Feste By'r lady,[34] sir, and some dogs will catch[35] well. 60

Sir Andrew Most certain. Let our catch be, "Thou knave."[36]

Feste "Hold thy peace, thou knave,"[37] knight? I shall be constrained[38] in't to call thee knave, knight.

Sir Andrew 'Tis not the first time I have constrained one[39] to call me knave. Begin, fool. It begins "Hold thy peace." 65

Feste I shall never begin if I hold my peace.

Sir Andrew Good,[40] i' faith. Come, begin.

CATCH SUNG

ENTER MARIA

Maria What a caterwauling[41] do you keep[42] here! If my lady have not called up her steward Malvolio and bid him turn you out of doors, never trust me. 70

Sir Toby My lady's a Cathayan,[43] we are politicians,[44] Malvolio's a Peg-a-Ramsey,[45] and "Three merry men be

---

32 weavers were noted for singing as they worked
33 experienced, adept
34 by'r lady = by Our Lady (Jesus' mother)
35 (1) capture, overtake, (2) seize
36 rascal, rogue*
37 a quotation from the song
38 obliged, compelled
39 someone
40 that's a good one / quip
41 the sounds of cats in the mating season
42 practice, perform
43 Chinaman, cheater ("Cathay")
44 schemers, plotters, intriguers
45 Peg-a-Ramsey = Margaret from Ramsey, a then-current song

we."[46] Am not I consanguineous?[47] Am I not of her blood?
Tillyvally,[48] lady, (*sings*) "There dwelt a man in Babylon, lady,
75   lady!"[49]

Feste   Beshrew me,[50] the knight's in admirable[51] fooling.

Sir Andrew   Ay, he does well enough if he be disposed,[52] and so
    do I too. He does it with a better grace, but I do it more
    natural.

80 *Sir Toby*   (*sings*) "O, the twelfth day of December" –

Maria   For the love o' God, peace!

ENTER MALVOLIO

Malvolio   My masters, are you mad? Or what are you? Have ye
    no wit, manners, nor honesty, but to gabble[53] like tinkers[54] at
    this time of night? Do ye make an alehouse[55] of my lady's
85   house, that ye squeak out your coziers'[56] catches without any
    mitigation or remorse[57] of voice? Is there no respect of place,
    persons, nor time in you?

46 a then-current song
47 related to her by blood
48 nonsense
49 "The Ballad of Constant Susanna": "There dwelt a man in Babylon / Of
   reputation great by fame; / He took to wife a fair womàn, / Susanna she was
   called by name: / A woman fair an virtuous; / Lady, lady; / Why should we
   not of her learn thus / To live godly?" (Thomas Percy, *Reliques of Ancient
   English Poetry*, vol. 1 [London: Routledge, 1996], 209–10)
50 beshrew me = may I be cursed (conventional exclamation)★
51 wonderful★
52 in the mood
53 jabber, chatter
54 craftsmen who repaired metal utensils and often went from place to place: of
   bad reputation for manners and morals
55 tavern
56 cobblers, shoemakers
57 mitigation or remorse = softening/limiting or hesitation/scruple/
   compassion

Sir Toby We did keep time, sir, in our catches. Sneck up![58]

Malvolio Sir Toby, I must be round[59] with you. My lady bade me
   tell you that, though she harbors[60] you as her kinsman, she's   90
   nothing allied to[61] your disorders.[62] If you can separate[63]
   yourself and your misdemeanors,[64] you are welcome to the
   house. If not, an it would please you to take leave of her, she is
   very willing to bid you farewell.

Sir Toby (*sings*) "Farewell, dear heart, since I must needs be   95
   gone."[65]

Maria Nay, good Sir Toby.

Feste (*sings*) "His eyes do show his days are almost done."

Malvolio Is't even so?[66]

Sir Toby (*sings*) "But I will never die."   100

Feste Sir Toby, there you lie.

Malvolio This is much credit to you.[67]

Sir Toby (*sings*) "Shall I bid him go?"

Feste (*sings*) "What an if[68] you do?"

Sir Toby (*sings*) "Shall I bid him go, and spare[69] not?"   105

Feste (*sings*) "O no, no, no, no, you dare not."

58 sneck up = lock it/shut up
59 precise, thorough
60 lodges, shelters
61 nothing allied to = has no kinship with
62 irregularities, disorderliness
63 disconnect
64 misconduct, evil behavior, offenses
65 Sir Toby and Feste adapt passages from the ballad "Corydon's Farewell to
   Phillis" (Percy, *Reliques of Ancient English Poetry,* 1:209–11)
66 "Is that how it is?"
67 "such behavior truly recommends you/adds to your good reputation"
68 what an if = and if
69 refrain

Sir Toby	(*to Malvolio*) Out o' tune[70] sir: ye lie. Art any more than a steward?[71] Dost thou think, because thou art virtuous, there shall be no more cakes[72] and ale?
110 *Feste*	Yes, by Saint Anne, and ginger[73] shall be hot i' the mouth too.
Sir Toby	(*to Feste*) Thou'rt i' the right. (*to Malvolio*) Go, sir, rub your chain with crumbs.[74] A stoup of wine, Maria!
Malvolio	Mistress Mary, if you prized[75] my lady's favor at
115	anything more than[76] contempt, you would not give means for[77] this uncivil rule.[78] She shall know of it, by this hand.[79]

EXIT MALVOLIO

Maria	(*calling after Malvolio*) Go shake your ears.[80]
Sir Andrew	'Twere as good a deed as to drink when a man's a-hungry,[81] to challenge him the field,[82] and then to break
120	promise with him[83] and make a fool of him.
Sir Toby	Do't knight, I'll write thee a challenge. Or I'll deliver thy indignation[84] to him by word of mouth.

---

70 out o' tune = you're (1) out of order/wrong, (2) in a bad mood/temper
71 household servant, supervising other servants
72 sweetened and flavored bread, often with nuts, raisins, etc.
73 used to spice ale
74 stewards wore decorative chains around their neck: Toby tells him to polish it with crumbs
75 valued
76 at anything more than = with anything more than
77 give means for = be an agent of/supporter for
78 uncivil rule = barbarous/unrefined/rude* practice/procedure
79 either (1) he will put it in writing, *or* (2) a rather tepid oath
80 i.e., he is a donkey
81 the proverbial saying, "that's as good a deed as to drink," is here mangled
82 challenge him the field = challenge him to a duel
83 i.e., not show up
84 anger, disdain, contempt

Maria   Sweet Sir Toby, be patient for tonight. Since[85] the
           youth of the Count's was today with thy lady, she is much out
           of quiet.[86] For Monsieur Malvolio, let[87] me alone with   125
           him.[88] If I do not gull[89] him into a nayword,[90] and make
           him a common recreation,[91] do not think I have wit enough
           to lie straight in my bed. I know I can do it.

Sir Toby   Possess[92] us, possess us, tell us something of him.

Maria   Marry, sir, sometimes he is a kind of Puritan.[93]   130

Sir Andrew O, if I thought that I'd beat him like a dog!

Sir Toby   What, for being a Puritan? Thy exquisite[94] reason,
           dear knight?

Sir Andrew I have no exquisite reason for't, but I have reason
           good enough.   135

Maria   The devil a Puritan that he is,[95] or anything
           constantly[96] but a time-pleaser,[97] an affectioned[98] ass, that
           cons state[99] without book and utters it by great swarths.[100]

85 after
86 tranquillity, calm
87 leave
88 i.e., let me handle this by myself★
89 deceive, fool, trick★
90 catchword, common saying
91 common recreation = universal/general amusement
92 inform, acquaint
93 Protestants who broke with the established Church of England; in
    Shakespeare's time, they were strict reformers, advocates of plainness,
    opponents of elaborate ceremony and rites
94 (1) ingenious, unusual, (2) carefully chosen, (3) exact
95 i.e., good Lord, he's not a real Puritan
96 loyally, faithfully, all the time
97 trimmer, sycophant
98 (1) self-willed, stubborn, (2) zealous, ambitious
99 status, standing, dignity
100 swaths, strips

The best persuaded[101] of himself. So crammed (as he thinks)
140   with excellencies, that it is his grounds of faith that all that
look on him love him. And on that vice[102] in him will my
revenge find notable[103] cause to work.

Sir Toby   What wilt thou do?

Maria   I will drop in his way some obscure epistles of love,
145   wherein by the color of his beard, the shape of his leg, the
manner of his gait, the expressure[104] of his eye, forehead,
and complexion, he shall find himself most feelingly
personated.[105] I can write very like my lady your niece. On
a forgotten matter we can hardly make distinction of our
150   hands.[106]

Sir Toby   Excellent, I smell a device.[107]

Sir Andrew   I have't in my nose too.

Sir Toby   He shall think, by the letters that thou wilt drop, that
they come from my niece, and that she's in love with him.

155 Maria   My purpose[108] is, indeed, a horse of that color.

Sir Andrew   And your horse now would make him an ass.

Maria   Ass, I doubt not.[109]

Sir Andrew   O 'twill be admirable!

Maria   Sport royal, I warrant[110] you. I know my physic[111]

---

101 having an assured opinion ("conceited")
102 moral fault/blemish/imperfection
103 excellent, remarkable★
104 expression
105 feelingly personated = forcefully/passionately represented
106 handwritings (i.e., dealing with a document we do not remember, neither
     of us can tell who wrote it)
107 plan, plot, scheme★
108 intention★
109 ass, I doubt not = (1) an ass, of course, *and* (2) you ass, of course
110 guarantee, promise★
111 medicine, purgative

will work with him. I will plant[112] you two, and let the   160
fool[113] make a third, where[114] he shall find the letter.
Observe his construction[115] of it. For this night, to bed, and
dream on[116] the event.[117] Farewell.

EXIT MARIA

Sir Toby	Good night, Penthesilea.[118]
Sir Andrew	Before me,[119] she's a good wench. 165
Sir Toby	She's a beagle,[120] true-bred,[121] and one that adores me. What o' that?[122]
Sir Andrew	I was adored once too.
Sir Toby	Let's to bed, knight. Thou hadst need[123] send for more money. 170
Sir Andrew	If I cannot recover[124] your niece, I am a foul way out.[125]
Sir Toby	Send for money, knight, if thou hast her not i' the end, call me cut.[126]

112 place
113 Malvolio
114 when
115 interpreting
116 of, about
117 actual happening, what it will be like when it happens
118 courageous queen of the Amazons, killed by Achilles (Maria is a very small
    woman) (PENthiSEELya)
119 before me = in my opinion/eyes (exclamation)
120 hound of small stature
121 a thoroughbred
122 so what?
123 better
124 get, win, obtain possession of
125 foul way out = bad/shameful/disgraceful manner out of pocket
126 a castrated horse ("gelding")

175 *Sir Andrew* If I do not, never trust me, take it how you will.

    Sir Toby Come, come, I'll go burn some sack.[127] 'Tis too late to go to bed now. Come knight, come knight.

EXEUNT

127 burn some sack = heat (with sugar in it) some white wine

SCENE 4

Duke Orsino's palace

ENTER ORSINO, VIOLA, CURIO, AND OTHERS

Orsino Give me some music. Now, good morrow, friends.
Now, good Cesario, but[1] that piece[2] of song,
That old and antic[3] song we heard last night.
Methought it did relieve my passion[4] much,
More than light airs and recollected terms[5]   5
Of these most brisk[6] and giddy-paced[7] times.
Come, but one verse.
Curio He is not here, so please your lordship that should[8]
sing it.
Orsino Who was it?   10
Curio Feste, the jester, my lord, a fool that the lady Olivia's
father took much delight in. He is about[9] the house.
Orsino Seek him out, and play the tune the while.

EXIT CURIO

MUSIC PLAYS

(to Viola) Come hither, boy. If ever thou shalt love,
In the sweet pangs of it remember me.   15

1 just
2 portion
3 bizarre, fantastic
4 suffering, affliction
5 recollected terms = polished/artificial/studied phrases/expressions/words
6 hasty, over-quick/active
7 giddy-paced = dizzily moving★
8 ought to
9 around, in

For such as I am all true lovers are,
Unstaid and skittish[10] in all motions[11] else,
Save in the constant image[12] of the creature
That is beloved. How dost thou like this tune?

20 *Viola* It gives a very echo to the seat[13]
Where Love is throned.

Orsino   Thou dost speak masterly.
My life upon't, young though thou art, thine eye
Hath stayed[14] upon some favor[15] that it loves.
Hath it not, boy?

Viola   A little, by your favor.[16]

Orsino What kind of woman is't?

25 *Viola*   Of your complexion.[17]

Orsino She is not worth thee, then. What years, i' faith?

Viola About your years, my lord.

Orsino Too old by heaven. Let still[18] the woman take
An elder than herself, so wears she[19] to him,

30 So sways[20] she level[21] in her husband's heart.
For boy, however we do praise ourselves,

---

10 unstaid and skittish = unrestrained/unregulated and changeable/difficult to
   deal with
11 emotions★
12 likeness, representation
13 place
14 paused, lingered, stopped
15 beauty, appearance, face★
16 by your favor = if you please, with your permission (conventional polite
   phrasing)
17 nature, disposition, character
18 always
19 wears she = forms herself
20 (1) moves, (2) rules★
21 steady

Our fancies are more giddy and unfirm,[22]
More longing,[23] wavering, sooner lost and worn,[24]
Than women's are.

Viola   I think it well, my lord.

Orsino Then let thy love be younger than thyself,   35
Or thy affection cannot hold the bent.[25]
For women are as roses, whose fair flower
Being once displayed,[26] doth fall that very hour.

Viola   And so they are. Alas that they are so.
To die,[27] even when they to perfection grow.   40

ENTER CURIO AND FESTE

Orsino O fellow come, the song we had last night.
Mark[28] it Cesario, it is old and plain.
The spinsters[29] and the knitters in the sun
And the free[30] maids that weave their thread with bones[31]   45
Do use[32] to chant it. It is silly sooth,[33]
And dallies with[34] the innocence of love,
Like the old age.[35]

22 flighty, unsteady
23 yearning
24 worn-out, enfeebled, exhausted
25 mental inclination
26 unfurled, spread open
27 expire (i.e., their beauty, not the women)
28 take note of, consider
29 spinners
30 unrestricted (because not yet married?)
31 bobbins made of trotter (horse's foot) bones (for weaving bonelace: a form of linen, knit to a pattern)
32 do use = are in the habit, customarily
33 silly sooth = simple/rustic truth
34 dallies with = speaks of, speaks/toys with
35 old age = former/old times

Feste   Are you ready, sir?

Orsino   Ay, prithee, sing.

MUSIC

Feste   (*sings*)

50   Come away,[36] come away death,
          And in sad cypress[37] let me be laid.
      Fly away, fly away breath,
          I am slain by a fair cruel maid.
      My shroud of white, stuck[38] all with yew,[39]
55   O prepare it!
      My part[40] of death, no one so true
              Did share it.
      Not a flower, not a flower sweet
      On my black coffin let there be strown.
60   Not a friend, not a friend greet[41]
      My poor corpse, where my bones shall be thrown.
          A thousand thousand sighs to save,[42]
          Lay me, O where
          Sad true lover never find my grave,
65   To weep there.

Orsino (*gives money*) There's for thy pains.

Feste   No pains sir, I take pleasure in singing, sir.

---

36 come away = hurry
37 sad cypress = trustworthy/enduring cypress wood (water-resistant;
    associated with funerals)
38 adorned, decorated, strewn
39 dark green foliage, symbolic of sadness/mourning
40 allotted portion/share
41 (1) pay respects to *or* (2) weep for
42 spare, make unnecessary

Orsino I'll pay thy pleasure then.

Feste   Truly, sir, and pleasure will be paid,[43] one time or
another.

Orsino Give me now leave to leave thee.[44]   70

Feste   Now the melancholy god protect thee, and the tailor
make thy doublet[45] of changeable[46] taffeta, for thy mind is a
very opal.[47] I would have men of such constancy[48] put to sea,
that their business might be everything, and their intent
everywhere, for that's it that[49] always makes a good voyage   75
of[50] nothing. Farewell.

EXIT FESTE

Orsino Let all the rest give place.[51]

CURIO AND ATTENDANTS RETIRE

Once more, Cesario,

Get[52] thee to yond same sovereign cruelty.[53]
Tell her[54] my love, more noble than the world,
Prizes not quantity of dirty lands.   80
The parts[55] that fortune hath bestowed upon her,

43 paid for
44 i.e., you may now leave
45 doublet = jacket-like garment, with or without sleeves
46 shot, changing color
47 gemstone in which color varies
48 determination, endurance
49 it that = what
50 out of
51 give place = withdraw, leave
52 go
53 (i.e., to Olivia)
54 tell her = tell her that
55 (1) share (inheritance, referring to the "dirty lands"), *or* (2) the qualities

Tell her I hold as giddily[56] as fortune.

But 'tis that miracle and queen of gems[57]

That nature pranks[58] her in attracts[59] my soul.

85 *Viola*   But if she cannot love you, sir?

Orsino   I cannot be so answered.[60]

Viola   Sooth, but you must.

Say[61] that some lady, as perhaps there is,

Hath for your love as great a pang[62] of heart

As you have for Olivia. You cannot love her.

90 You tell her so. Must she not then be answered?

Orsino   There is no woman's sides[63]

Can bide the beating of so strong a passion

As love doth give my heart. No woman's heart

So big, to hold so much, they lack retention.[64]

95 Alas, their love may be called appetite,

No motion of the liver, but the palate,[65]

That suffer surfeit, cloyment, and revolt.[66]

But mine is all as hungry as the sea,

And can digest as much. Make no compare

100 Between that love a woman can bear me,

And that I owe Olivia.

56 carelessly, indifferently
57 (i.e., her beauty)
58 dresses, decks, adorns
59 which attracts
60 satisfied ("paid")
61 suppose
62 intense mental anguish
63 ribs, body
64 memory
65 what the mouth can't taste
66 suffer surfeit, cloyment, and revolt = suffers disorder from excessive intake, satiety/satiation, and protest/withdrawal/revulsion

Viola   Ay, but I know –

Orsino   What dost thou know?

Viola   Too well what love women to men may owe.[67]

In faith, they are as true of heart as we.

My father had a daughter loved a man   105

As it might be, perhaps, were I a woman,

I should your lordship.

Orsino   And what's her history?[68]

Viola   A blank, my lord. She never told her love,

But let concealment like a worm i' the bud

Feed on her damask[69] cheek. She pined in thought,   110

And with a green and yellow[70] melancholy

She sat like patience on a monument,[71]

Smiling at grief. Was not this love indeed?

We men may say more, swear more, but indeed

Our shows[72] are more than will.[73] For still[74] we prove   115

Much in our vows, but little in our love.

Orsino   But died thy sister of her love, my boy?

Viola   I am all the daughters of my father's house,

And all the brothers too. And yet[75] I know not.

Sir, shall I to this lady?

67 possess, own
68 story
69 the pinkish color of a damask rose
70 green and yellow: i.e., indicative of melancholy, green/bile and yellow/sickly/pale
71 patience on a monument = a statuary representation of Patience on a sepulcher/tomb
72 actions, displays★
73 our will/desire
74 always
75 as yet

120 *Orsino*   Ay, that's the theme.
      To her in haste. Give her this jewel. Say,
      My love can give no place,[76] bide no denay.[77]

76 give no place = give way, yield
77 denial

SCENE 5

Olivia's garden

ENTER SIR TOBY BELCH, SIR ANDREW, AND FABIAN

Sir Toby   Come thy ways,[1] Signior Fabian.

Fabian   Nay,[2] I'll come. If I lose a scruple[3] of this sport, let
me be boiled[4] to death with melancholy.

Sir Toby   Wouldst thou not be glad to have the niggardly[5]
rascally sheep-biter[6] come by some notable shame?   5

Fabian   I would exult, man. You know he brought me[7] out
o' favor with my lady about a bear-baiting here.

Sir Toby   To anger him we'll have the bear again, and we will
fool him black and blue,[8] shall we not, Sir Andrew?

Sir Andrew An we do not, it is pity of our lives.   10

Sir Toby   Here comes the little villain.[9]

ENTER MARIA

How now, my metal of India![10]

Maria   Get ye all three into the box-tree.[11] Malvolio's
coming down this walk, he has been yonder i' the sun
practicing behavior to his own shadow this half hour.   15

1 come thy ways = come along, come
2 here, an exclamation, *not* a negation
3 small measurement ("twentie barley cornes")★
4 pronounced BILED, which closely ties it to liver bile, yellowish and causing
peevishness, etc.
5 stingy, close-fisted, miserly
6 sneak (like a dog that sneaks into the fold and worries/bites sheep)
7 brought me = caused me to be
8 i.e., figuratively, not literally, "beat" him
9 used here in fun
10 i.e., gold
11 cluster of small evergreen shrubs

Observe him, for the love of mockery, for I know this letter
will make a contemplative[12] idiot of him. Close,[13] in the
name of jesting. (*they hide*) Lie thou there, (*throws down a letter*)
for here comes the trout that must be caught with tickling.[14]

EXIT MARIA

ENTER MALVOLIO

20   *Malvolio*   'Tis but fortune, all is fortune. Maria once told me
she[15] did affect[16] me, and I have heard herself come thus
near,[17] that[18] should she fancy,[19] it should be one of my
complexion. Besides, she uses[20] me with a more exalted[21]
respect than any one else that follows[22] her. What should I
25   think on't?[23]

   Sir Toby   Here's an overweening[24] rogue.

   Fabian   O peace. Contemplation[25] makes a rare turkey-
cock[26] of him. How he jets[27] under his advanced plumes.[28]

12 thoughtful, reflective
13 hide
14 craving, hankering
15 Olivia
16 did affect = was drawn to/fond of
17 close
18 saying that
19 take a fancy to someone
20 treats
21 lofty, elevated
22 serves, attends on
23 about it
24 someone who is presumptuous/arrogant/conceited (a "show-off")
25 musing, considered thought
26 i.e., swelling up
27 swaggers, struts
28 advanced plumes = raised feathers

Sir Andrew	'Slight,[29] I could so[30] beat the rogue!	
Sir Toby	Peace, I say.	30
Malvolio	To be Count Malvolio!	
Sir Toby	Ah, rogue!	
Sir Andrew	Pistol him, pistol him.	
Sir Toby	Peace, peace!	
Malvolio	There is example for't. The lady of the Strachy[31]	35

married the yeoman[32] of the wardrobe.

Sir Andrew Fie on him, Jezebel![33]

Fabian O peace! Now he's deeply in.[34] Look how
imagination blows[35] him.

Malvolio Having been three months married to her, sitting in   40
  my state −

Sir Toby O for a stone-bow,[36] to hit him in the eye!

Malvolio Calling my officers[37] about me, in my branched[38]
velvet gown, having come from a day-bed,[39] where I have
left Olivia sleeping −   45

Sir Toby Fire and brimstone!

Fabian O peace, peace!

Malvolio And then to have the humor[40] of state. And after a

29 God's light (mild exclamation)★
30 indeed
31 the allusion is not understood, but the sense is clear: a female aristocrat who
   marries someone of lower class standing
32 high-ranking servant
33 the proud, wicked queen of Israel's King Ahab (1 Kings 16:31)
34 into it
35 drives/inflames/inflates him, makes him bluster/brag
36 crossbow that shoots stones
37 agents, ministers
38 embroidery-adorned
39 sofa
40 spirit (i.e., looking important)

demure travel of regard,[41] telling them I know my place as I
would they should do theirs. To ask for my kinsman Toby –

Sir Toby   Bolts and shackles![42]

Fabian   O peace, peace, peace! Now, now.

Malvolio Seven of my people, with an obedient start,[43] make
out[44] for him. I frown the while, and perchance wind up my
watch, or play with my (*reaches for his steward's chain, and stops
himself*) – some rich jewel. Toby approaches, curtsies[45] there
to me –

Sir Toby   Shall this fellow live?

Fabian   Though our silence be drawn from us with cars,[46] yet
peace.

Malvolio I extend my hand to him thus, quenching my
familiar[47] smile with an austere[48] regard of control[49] –

Sir Toby   And does not Toby take[50] you a blow o' the lips then?

Malvolio Saying, "Cousin Toby, my fortunes[51] having cast[52] me
on your niece, give me this prerogative[53] of speech" –

Sir Toby   What, what?

41 demure travel of regard = calm/sober/composed look★ of inspection (of
  his servants)
42 bolts and shackles = fetters and wrist-ankle-fetters (i.e., put him in chains, as
  a criminal)
43 hurry, rush, leap
44 make out = go forth
45 makes a sign of reverence (bows?)
46 wagons, chariots, etc.
47 intimate
48 rigorous, stern
49 command
50 catch ("give"), strike
51 prosperity, good luck
52 bestowed
53 right, privilege

Malvolio	"You must amend your drunkenness."
Sir Toby	Out, scab![54]
Fabian	Nay, patience, or we break the sinews[55] of our plot. 70
Malvolio	"Besides, you waste the treasure of your time with a foolish knight" –
Sir Andrew	That's me, I warrant you.
Malvolio	"One Sir Andrew" –
Sir Andrew	I knew 'twas I, for many do call me fool. 75
Malvolio	What employment[56] have we here?

PICKING UP THE LETTER

Fabian	Now is the woodcock[57] near the gin.[58]
Sir Toby	O peace! And[59] the spirit of humour intimate[60] reading aloud to him.
Malvolio	By my life this is my lady's hand. These be her very 80 C's, her U's, and her T's, and thus makes she her great[61] P's. It is in contempt of question[62] her hand.
Sir Andrew	Her C's, her U's and her T's.[63] Why that?
Malvolio	(*reads*) "To the unknown[64] beloved, this, and my good wishes." Her very phrases! (*to the seal*) By your leave, 85

54 scabies or other skin disease ("scoundrel, rascal")
55 connective cords
56 business
57 snipe-like bird*
58 snare, trap
59 and may
60 (verb) suggest
61 capital
62 in contempt of question = further inquiry would be worthless
63 i.e., he hears "seas," "ewes," and "teas"
64 unknowing

wax. Soft![65] And the impressure[66] her Lucrece,[67] with which
she uses to seal.[68] 'Tis my lady. To whom should this be?

Fabian   This wins him, liver and all.

Malvolio (*reads*)

90   Jove knows I love.

          But who?

          Lips, do not move.

          No man must know.

"No man must know." What follows? The numbers[69] altered!

95   "No man must know." If this should be thee, Malvolio?[70]

Toby   Marry, hang thee, brock![71]

Malvolio (*reads*)

          I may command where I adore,

              But silence, like a Lucrece knife,

100   With bloodless stroke my heart doth gore.

              M, O, A, I, doth sway my life.

Fabian   A fustian[72] riddle.

Sir Toby   Excellent wench, say I.

Malvolio   "M, O, A, I, doth sway my life." Nay, but first, let me

105   see, let me see, let me see.

Fabian   What dish o' poison has she dressed[73] him!

---

65 slow, slow
66 impression on the wax
67 Roman lady, who committed suicide after being raped by Emperor
   Tarquinius
68 uses to = customarily seals with wax
69 meter (i.e., he observes that lines 1, 3, and 4 have two prosodic feet, but line 2
   has only one)
70 malVOWleeOW: does he perhaps say it thus? Or malVOWlyow?
71 skunk, dirty fellow
72 bombastic, turgid, inflated (i.e., as required for a fustian man)
73 prepared for

Sir Toby   And with what wing[74] the staniel checks[75] at it!

Malvolio   "I may command where I adore." Why, she may
  command me. I serve her, she is my lady. Why, this is evident
  to any formal capacity.[76] There is no obstruction in this. And   110
  the end – what should[77] that alphabetical position[78]
  portend,[79] if I could make that resemble something in me.
  Softly, M, O, A, I.

Sir Toby   O ay, make up[80] that. He is now at a cold scent.

Fabian   Sowter[81] will cry upon't for all[82] this, though it be as   115
  rank[83] as a fox.

Malvolio   M. Malvolio. M. Why, that begins my name.

Fabian   Did not I say he would work it out? The cur is
  excellent at faults.[84]

Malvolio   M. But then there is no consonancy[85] in the sequel.   120
  That suffers under probation.[86] A should follow, but O does.

Fabian   And O[87] shall end, I hope.

Sir Toby   Ay, or I'll cudgel him, and make him cry O!

Malvolio   And then I comes behind.

Fabian   Ay, and you had any eye behind you, you might see   125

74 what wing: i.e., how the bird approaches the intended prey – here, the
  wrong one
75 staniel checks = kestrel (hawk useless for hunting) strikes
76 formal capacity = ordinary/conventional/basic ability★
77 must
78 arrangement
79 point to, indicate, mean
80 make up = fill up, complete, fit together
81 a hunting dog's name (literally, "cobbler, shoemaker")
82 cry upon't for all = yelp at it despite
83 gross/obvious
84 scents that have gone cold
85 agreement, harmony ("sequence")
86 suffers under probation = resists/needs investigation/examination
87 (?) if "O" ends him, it could refer to a hangman's noose

more detraction[88] at your heels than fortunes before you.

Malvolio M, O, A, I. This simulation[89] is not as the former. And
yet, to crush[90] this a little, it would[91] bow to me, for every
one of these letters are in my name. Soft, here follows prose.

130 *(reads)* "If this fall into thy hand, revolve.[92] In my stars I am
above thee, but be not afraid of greatness. Some are born
great, some achieve greatness, and some have greatness thrust
upon 'em. Thy Fates open their hands,[93] let thy blood and
spirit[94] embrace them, and to inure[95] thyself to what thou art

135 like to be, cast thy humble slough[96] and appear fresh.[97] Be
opposite[98] with a kinsman, surly with servants. Let thy
tongue tang[99] arguments of state, put thyself into the trick of
singularity.[100] She thus advises thee that sighs for thee.
Remember who commended thy yellow stockings, and

140 wished to see thee ever cross-gartered.[101] I say remember, go
to,[102] thou art made, if thou desirest to be so. If not, let me see
thee a steward still, the fellow of servants, and not worthy to
touch Fortune's fingers. Farewell. She that would alter

---

88 loss of reputation
89 false appearance/imitation
90 squeeze
91 should
92 consider, ponder
93 i.e., destiny is offering its generosity to you
94 blood and spirit = passion and vitality/life-force
95 accustom
96 outer skin (SLUFF)
97 anew
98 contrary, antagonistic, hostile
99 strike with a ringing tone
100 trick of singularity = (1) appearance, (2) frolic/roguery of uniqueness/
     individuality/differentness
101 garters worn crossed/slanted (like an X)
102 get to work, hurry

services[103] with thee, The Fortunate Unhappy." Daylight and
champaign discovers[104] not more. This is open. I will be   145
proud, I will read politic[105] authors, I will baffle[106] Sir Toby, I
will wash off gross acquaintance,[107] I will be point-device,[108]
the very man. I do not now fool myself, to let imagination
jade[109] me, for every reason excites[110] to this, that my lady
loves me. She did commend my yellow stockings of late, she   150
did praise my leg being cross-gartered, and in this she
manifests[111] herself to my love, and with a kind of
injunction[112] drives me to these habits[113] of her liking. I
thank my stars, I am happy. I will be strange,[114] stout,[115] in
yellow stockings, and cross-gartered, even with the swiftness   155
of putting on.[116] Jove and my stars be praised! Here is yet a
postscript. (*reads*) "Thou canst not choose but know who I
am. If thou entertainest my love, let it appear in thy smiling,
thy smiles become thee well. Therefore in my presence still[117]
smile, dear my sweet, I prithee." Jove, I thank thee, I will smile,   160
I will do everything that thou wilt have me.[118]

103 duties
104 champaign discovers = open country reveals
105 judicious, prudent, sagacious
106 (1) disgrace, (2) condescend to
107 gross acquaintance = coarse/rough/dull friends
108 exactly right, perfect in every way
109 make a fool of
110 points, moves toward
111 reveals
112 emphatic command
113 (1) clothing, (2) behaviors*
114 different, unusual, out of the way, extreme
115 arrogant, haughty
116 putting on = (1) getting started, urging on,* (2) dressing myself thus
117 always
118 me do

EXIT MALVOLIO

Fabian   I will not give my part of this sport for a pension of
thousands to be paid from the Sophy.[119]

Sir Toby   I could marry this wench for this device.

165 *Sir Andrew* So could I too.

Sir Toby   And ask no other dowry[120] with her but such
another jest.

Sir Andrew Nor I neither.

Fabian   Here comes my noble gull-catcher.

ENTER MARIA

170 *Sir Toby*   Wilt thou set thy foot o' my neck?[121]

Sir Andrew Or o' mine either?

Sir Toby   Shall I play[122] my freedom at traytrip,[123] and
become thy bond-slave?

Sir Andrew I' faith, or I either?

175 *Sir Toby*   Why, thou hast put him in such a dream, that when
the image of it leaves him he must run mad.

Maria   Nay but say true, does it work upon him?

Sir Toby   Like aqua-vitae[124] with a midwife.

Maria   If you will then see the fruits of the sport, mark his
180   first approach before my lady. He will come to her in yellow
stockings, and 'tis a color she abhors, and cross-gartered, a
fashion she detests. And he will smile upon her, which will

119 the Shah (Persian king)★
120 money/property transferred to the husband from the wife, at the time of
marriage
121 in triumph (like a gladiator)
122 gamble
123 dice game ("trey-trip": trey = two)
124 highly distilled/very strong liquor ("water of life")

now be so unsuitable to her disposition, being addicted to a
melancholy as she is, that it cannot but turn him into a
notable contempt.[125] If you will see it, follow me.   185

Sir Toby   To the gates of Tartar,[126] thou most excellent devil
of wit!

Sir Andrew I'll make one[127] too.

EXEUNT

125 condition of being despised
126 Tartarus, Hell
127 make one = join in

Act 3

❦

Olivia's garden

ENTER VIOLA, AND FESTE WITH A TABOR[1]

Viola Save[2] thee, friend, and thy music. Dost thou live by[3] thy
  tabor?

Feste No sir, I live by[4] the church.

Viola Art thou a churchman?

5 *Feste* No such matter,[5] sir. I do live by the church, for I do live
  at my house, and my house doth stand by the church.

Viola So thou mayst say, the king lies by[6] a beggar, if a beggar
  dwell near him. Or the church stands by[7] thy tabor, if thy
  tabor stand by the church.

---

1 small drum
2 may God save★
3 by means of
4 near
5 thing
6 sleeps with
7 stands by = (1) supports, protects, (2) rests/depends upon

74

Feste You have said, sir. To see[8] this age! A sentence is but a   10
cheveril[9] glove to a good wit. How quickly the wrong side
may be turned outward.

Viola Nay, that's certain. They that dally nicely[10] with words
may quickly make them wanton.[11]

Feste I would, therefore, my sister had had no name, sir.   15

Viola Why man?

Feste Why sir, her name's a word, and to dally with that word
might make my sister wanton. But indeed words are very
rascals, since bonds[12] disgraced them.

Viola Thy reason, man?   20

Feste Troth sir, I can yield[13] you none without words, and
words are grown so false, I am loath to prove reason with
them.

Viola I warrant thou art a merry fellow and carest for nothing.

Feste Not so sir, I do care for something. But in my   25
conscience,[14] sir, I do not care for you. If that be to care for
nothing, sir, I would[15] it would make you invisible.

Viola Art not thou the Lady Olivia's fool?

Feste No indeed sir, the Lady Olivia has no folly, she will keep
no fool sir, till she be married, and fools are as like husbands as   30
pilchards[16] are to herrings, the husband's the bigger. I am
indeed not her fool, but her corrupter of words.

---

8 to see = just consider
9 soft kidskin
10 dally nicely = play elegantly / daintily / pleasantly
11 rebellious, undisciplined, naughty
12 security pledges (pun on "A man's word is his bond"?)
13 render, give★
14 heart
15 wish
16 smaller, rounder species of herring

Viola I saw thee late at the Count Orsino's.

Feste Foolery sir, does walk about the orb[17] like the sun, it
35   shines everywhere. I would be sorry sir, but the fool should[18]
      be as oft with your master as with my mistress. I think I saw
      your wisdom there.

Viola Nay, an thou pass upon[19] me, I'll no more with thee.
      Hold,[20] there's expenses for thee.

40 *Feste* Now Jove, in his next commodity[21] of hair, send thee a
      beard!

Viola By my troth, I'll tell thee, I am almost sick for one,[22]
      (*aside*) though I would not have it grow on my chin. Is thy
      lady within?

45 *Feste* Would not a pair of these[23] have bred, sir?

Viola Yes, being kept together and put to use.

Feste I would play Lord Pandarus[24] of Phrygia sir, to bring a
      Cressida to this Troilus.

Viola I understand you sir. (*giving him more money*) 'Tis well
50   begged.

Feste The matter, I hope, is not great sir, begging but a beggar.[25]
      Cressida was a beggar.[26] My lady is within sir. I will conster[27]

---

17 earth, world
18 ought to
19 (?) run / hit at? impose upon? make a fool of?
20 stop, wait★
21 shipment, consignment
22 for one = over one (Orsino)
23 i.e., Viola has given him two coins; he tries to turn two into more
24 the licentious go-between in Geoffrey Chaucer's *Troilus and Criseyde* and
    Shakespeare's *Troilus and Cressida*
25 i.e., since the person begging (himself) is no more than a beggar
26 not in Chaucer but in Robert Henryson's "The Testament of Cresseid"
    (ca. 1505), in which the gods decree, "This sall [thus must] thow [you] go
    begging fra [from] house to house" (line 342)
27 construe, explain

to them whence you come. Who you are and what you
would are out of my welkin, I might say "element," but the
word is overworn.   55

EXIT FESTE

Viola   This fellow is wise enough to play the fool,
            And to do that well craves a kind of wit.
            He must observe their mood on whom he jests,
            The quality of persons, and the time,
            And like the haggard,[28] check at every feather   60
            That comes before his eye. This is a practice
            As full of labor as a wise man's art.
            For folly, that he wisely shows is fit,[29]
            But wise men, folly-fall'n, quite taint[30] their wit.

ENTER SIR TOBY, AND SIR ANDREW

Sir Toby   Save you, gentleman.   65
Viola   And you, sir.
Sir Andrew   *Dieu vous garde, monsieur*.[31]
Viola   *Et vous aussi. Vôtre serviteur*.[32]
Sir Andrew   I hope sir, you are, and I am yours.
Sir Toby   Will you encounter[33] the house? My niece is   70
            desirous you should enter, if your trade[34] be to her.
Viola   I am bound[35] to your niece, sir. I mean, she is the

---

28 hawk
29 suitable, appropriate
30 quite taint = completely injure / tarnish / ruin the reputation of ★
31 may God protect you, sir
32 and you too. Your servant, sir.
33 approach (high-falutin' style)
34 business
35 headed

list[36] of my voyage.

Sir Toby   Taste[37] your legs sir, put them to motion.

75   Viola   My legs do better understand[38] me sir, than I
understand what you mean by bidding me taste my legs.

Sir Toby   I mean, to go sir, to enter.

Viola   I will answer you with gait and entrance. But we are
prevented.[39]

ENTER OLIVIA AND MARIA

80   Most excellent accomplished[40] lady, the heavens rain odors[41]
on you!

Sir Andrew That youth's a rare courtier. "Rain odors," well.[42]

Viola   My matter hath no voice, to[43] your own most
pregnant and vouchsafed[44] ear.

85   Sir Andrew "Odors," "pregnant," and "vouchsafed." I'll get 'em
all three all ready.

Olivia   Let the garden door be shut, and leave me to my
hearing.[45]

EXEUNT SIR TOBY, SIR ANDREW, AND MARIA

Give me your hand, sir.

90   Viola   My duty,[46] madam, and most humble service.

36 (1) pleasure, inclination, (2) region, territory, (3) direction
37 try, test★
38 stand underneath *and* comprehend
39 anticipated
40 perfect
41 sweet fragrance, perfume
42 very good, well done
43 except to
44 gracious
45 listening, audience
46 homage, due respect

Olivia What is your name?

Viola Cesario is your servant's name, fair princess.

Olivia My servant, sir? 'Twas never merry world
　　Since lowly feigning[47] was called compliment.
　　You're servant to the Count Orsino, youth.　　　　　　　　95

Viola And he is yours, and his must needs be yours.
　　Your servant's servant is your servant, madam.

Olivia For him, I think not on him. For his[48] thoughts,
　　Would they were blanks rather than filled with me.

Viola Madam, I come to whet[49] your gentle thoughts　　　100
　　On his behalf.

Olivia　　　　　　O by your leave, I pray you,
　　I bade you never speak again of him.
　　But would you undertake[50] another suit,[51]
　　I had rather hear you to solicit that
　　Than music from the spheres.[52]　　　　　　　　　　105

Viola　　　　　　　　　　　　Dear lady –

Olivia Give me leave, beseech you. I did send,
　　After the last enchantment[53] you did here,
　　A ring in chase[54] of you. So did I abuse[55]
　　Myself, my servant and, I fear me, you.
　　Under your hard construction[56] must I sit,　　　　　　110

47 lowly feigning = put-on/assumed lowness/baseness
48 for him . . . for his = as for him . . . as for his
49 urge on ("sharpen")
50 would you undertake = if you wish to venture/enter on
51 i.e., a proposal of marriage
52 i.e., celestial harmonies
53 overwhelming charm
54 pursuit
55 deceive★
56 hard construction = harsh/severe interpretation, explanation

To force that[57] on you, in a shameful cunning,
Which you knew none of yours. What might you think?
Have you not set[58] mine honor at the stake
And baited it with all the unmuzzled[59] thoughts
115   That tyrannous[60] heart can think? To one of your receiving[61]
Enough is shown. A cypress,[62] not a bosom,
Hideth my heart. So, let me hear you speak.

Viola   I pity you.

Olivia   That's a degree to love.

Viola   No, not a grize,[63] for 'tis a vulgar proof[64]
120   That very oft we pity enemies.

Olivia   Why then, methinks 'tis time to smile again.
O world, how apt the poor are to be proud!
If one should be a prey, how much the better
To fall before the lion than the wolf. (*clock strikes*)
125   The clock upbraids[65] me with the waste of time.
Be not afraid, good youth, I will not have[66] you.
And yet, when wit and youth is come to harvest,
Your wife is alike to reap a proper man.
There lies your way, due west.

130 *Viola*   Then westward-ho![67] Grace and good disposition

57 the ring
58 been setting (all this time)
59 free, unrestricted (as the dogs are unmuzzled, in bear-baiting)
60 despotic, severe, relentless
61 understanding
62 black transparent cloth, crape
63 single step
64 vulgar proof = common fact
65 censures, reproaches
66 (1) hold, retain, (2) press, take advantage of
67 let's sail (cry of ferrymen taking passengers from London to the court at Westminster)

Attend your ladyship!

You'll nothing, madam, to my lord by me?

Olivia Stay:

I prithee, tell me what thou thinkest of me.

Viola   That you do think you are not what you are.   135

Olivia   If I think so, I think the same of you.

Viola   Then think you right. I am not what I am.

Olivia   I would you were as I would have you be.

Viola   Would it be better, madam, than I am?

I wish it might, for now I am your fool.[68]   140

Olivia   (*aside*) O what a deal of scorn looks beautiful

In the contempt and anger of his lip!

A murderous guilt shows not itself more soon

Than love that would seem hid. Love's night is noon.[69]

(*aloud*) Cesario, by the roses of the spring,   145

By maidhood, honor, truth, and everything,

I love thee so, that, maugre[70] all thy pride,

Nor wit nor reason can my passion hide.

Do not extort thy reasons from this clause,

For that[71] I woo, thou therefore hast no cause,[72]   150

But rather reason thus with reason fetter.[73]

Love sought is good, but given unsought is better.

Viola   By innocence I swear, and by my youth,

I have one heart, one bosom, and one truth,

---

68 i.e., you are fooling/toying with me
69 i.e., the clarity of noon is fatal ("dark") to love
70 despite
71 because
72 reason to love
73 instead, you bind/enchain my reason (for loving you) with reason (your reason for not loving me)

155   And that no woman has, nor never none
       Shall mistress be of it, save I alone.
       And so adieu, good madam. Never more
       Will I my master's tears to you deplore.[74]
   Olivia Yet come again, for thou perhaps mayst move
160   That heart, which now abhors, to like his love.

EXEUNT

74 bewail, grieve over

SCENE 2
Olivia's house

ENTER SIR TOBY, SIR ANDREW, AND FABIAN

Sir Andrew No, faith, I'll not stay a jot[1] longer.

Sir Toby   Thy reason, dear venom,[2] give thy reason.

Fabian   You must needs yield your reason, Sir Andrew.

Sir Andrew Marry, I saw your niece do more favors to the
Count's servingman than ever she bestowed upon me. I saw't   5
i' the orchard.[3]

Sir Toby   Did she see thee the while, old boy? Tell me that.

Sir Andrew As plain as I see you now.

Fabian   This was a great argument[4] of love in her toward
you.   10

Sir Andrew 'Slight, will you make an ass o' me?

Fabian   I will prove it legitimate,[5] sir, upon the oaths of[6]
judgment and reason.

Sir Toby   And they have been grand-jurymen[7] since before
Noah was a sailor.   15

Fabian   She did show favor to the youth in your sight only to
exasperate you, to awake your dormouse[8] valor, to put fire in
your heart and brimstone in your liver. You should then have
accosted[9] her, and with some excellent jests, fire-new from

1 a jot = the least/smallest bit★
2 baleful/sinful/envious friend
3 garden
4 proof, evidence, manifestation
5 genuine, real, logical
6 oaths of = appeals to
7 jury of inquiry (rather than a trial jury)
8 sleepy, dozing ("hibernating")
9 approached

20   the mint, you should have banged[10] the youth into
      dumbness. This was looked for at your hand, and this was
      balked.[11] The double gilt[12] of this opportunity you let time
      wash off, and you are now sailed into the north of my lady's
      opinion, where you will hang like an icicle on a Dutchman's
25   beard,[13] unless you do redeem[14] it by some laudable attempt,
      either of valor or policy.[15]

Sir Andrew   An't be any way, it must be with valor, for policy I
      hate. I had as lief[16] be a Brownist[17] as a politician.

Sir Toby   Why then, build me[18] thy fortunes upon the basis of
30   valor. Challenge me the Count's youth to fight with him,
      hurt[19] him in eleven places, my niece shall take note[20] of it,
      and assure thyself, there is no love-broker in the world can
      more prevail in man's commendation[21] with woman than
      report of valor.

35 *Fabian*   There is no way but this, Sir Andrew.

Sir Andrew   Will either of you bear me a challenge to him?

Sir Toby   Go, write it in a martial hand, be curst[22] and brief. It
      is no matter how witty, so it be eloquent[23] and full of

---

10 thrashed
11 missed, omitted, passed over
12 gold-plating
13 William Barnetz, a Dutchman, explored Arctic waters in 1596–97; an
   account of the voyage was published in 1598
14 recover, regain
15 skill, cunning ("diplomacy")
16 as lief = rather, prefer
17 Robert Browne, Puritan-minded ecclesiastical reformer
18 build me = build
19 hit, wound
20 notice, attention★
21 recommendation, approval
22 disagreeable, virulent, fierce
23 powerfully fluent

invention.[24] Taunt him with the licence[25] of ink. If thou
thou'st[26] him some thrice, it shall not be amiss, and as many   40
lies as will lie in thy sheet of paper, although the sheet were
big enough for the bed of Ware[27] in England, set 'em down,
go about it. Let there be gall[28] enough in thy ink, though
thou write with a goose-pen,[29] no matter. About it.

Sir Andrew Where shall I find you?   45

Sir Toby We'll call thee at the cubiculo.[30] Go.

EXIT SIR ANDREW

Fabian This is a dear manikin[31] to you, Sir Toby.

Sir Toby I have been dear[32] to him, lad, some two thousand
strong,[33] or so.

Fabian We shall have a rare letter from him. But you'll not   50
deliver't?

Sir Toby Never trust me,[34] then. And by all means stir[35] on
the youth to an answer. I think oxen and wainropes[36] cannot
hale them[37] together. For Andrew, if he were opened,[38] and

24 fabrication, contrivance, imagination★
25 liberty
26 i.e., use the familiar second person singular "thou," rather than the more
   formal second person plural "you"
27 10′ 9″ square
28 bile
29 (1) goose-feather pen, (2) fool's pen
30 the cubiculo = your bedchamber
31 dear manikin = glorious little man/pygmy/puppet
32 expensive
33 worth (2,000 pounds was then a fortune)
34 never trust me = you had better believe I will ("if I don't, never trust me
   again")
35 agitate, impel, rouse
36 cart-ropes (i.e., heavy ropes)
37 draw, pull
38 cut open (as in an autopsy)

55   you find so much blood in his liver as will clog[39] the foot of a
flea, I'll eat the rest of the anatomy.[40]

Fabian   And his opposite,[41] the youth, bears in his visage[42] no
great presage[43] of cruelty.

ENTER MARIA

Sir Toby   Look, where the youngest wren[44] of mine comes.

60   *Maria*   If you desire the spleen,[45] and will[46] laugh yourself into
stitches,[47] follow me. Yond gull Malvolio is turned heathen, a
very renegado,[48] for there is no Christian, that[49] means to be
saved by believing rightly, can ever believe such impossible
passages[50] of grossness. He's in yellow stockings.

65   *Sir Toby*   And cross-gartered?

Maria   Most villanously.[51] Like a pedant[52] that keeps[53] a
school i' the church. I have dogged[54] him, like[55] his murderer.
He does obey every point of the letter that I dropped to
betray him. He does smile his face into more lines than is in

39 fill up
40 body
41 opponent, antagonist★
42 countenance, face
43 sign, indication, portent
44 small bird
45 considered the site of laughter/mirth
46 wish to
47 pains in the sides
48 renegade (commonly applied to Christians who convert to Islam)
49 who
50 possibilities
51 atrociously, detestably, vilely
52 teacher (negative)
53 conducts, takes care of
54 tracked, followed
55 as if I were

the new map with the augmentation[56] of the Indies.[57] You   70
have not seen such a thing as 'tis. I can hardly forbear[58]
hurling things at him. I know my lady will strike him. If she
do, he'll smile and take't for a great favor.

Sir Toby Come, bring us, bring us where he is.

EXEUNT

56 enlargement, addition
57 Richard Hakluyt's 1600 map
58 refrain/keep myself from

SCENE 3

A street

ENTER SEBASTIAN AND ANTONIO

Sebastian I would not by my will have troubled you,
But since you make your pleasure of your pains,
I will no further chide[1] you.

Antonio I could not stay behind you. My desire[2]
5 (More sharp than filèd steel) did spur me forth,
And not all love[3] to see you (though[4] so much
As might have drawn one to a longer voyage),
But jealousy[5] what might befall[6] your travel,
Being[7] skilless in these parts, which to a stranger,
10 Unguided and unfriended, often prove
Rough[8] and unhospitable. My willing love,
The rather[9] by these arguments of fear,
Set forth in your pursuit.

Sebastian   My kind Antonio,
I can no other answer make but thanks,
15 And thanks. And ever oft good turns[10]
Are shuffled[11] off with such uncurrent[12] pay:

1 scold, reprove
2 emotion, wish, desire
3 sympathy, affection (friendship was as important as sex)
4 though that is
5 anxiety/solicitude★
6 happen★ during
7 you being
8 harsh, disagreeable, violent★
9 the rather = all the sooner/quicker
10 deeds
11 evaded
12 unrecognized ("not in commercial circulation")

But were my worth,[13] as is my conscience, firm,
You should find better dealing.[14] What's to do?
Shall we go see the reliques[15] of this town?

Antonio Tomorrow, sir. Best first go see your lodging.   20

Sebastian I am not weary, and 'tis long to night.
I pray you, let us satisfy our eyes
With the memorials and the things of fame
That do renown[16] this city.

Antonio   Would[17] you'd pardon me.
I do not without danger walk these streets.   25
Once, in a sea-fight 'gainst the Count his galleys,[18]
I did some service,[19] of such note[20] indeed,
That were I ta'en[21] here it would scarce be answered.[22]

Sebastian Belike[23] you slew great number of his people.

Antonio The offense[24] is not of such a bloody nature,   30
Albeit[25] the quality[26] of the time and quarrel
Might well have given us bloody argument.
It might have since been answered in repaying
What we took from them, which for traffic's[27] sake,

13 possessions, property, means
14 treatment
15 relics
16 celebrate, make famous
17 I wish
18 the Count his galleys = Duke Orsino's ships
19 work
20 quality, distinguishing characteristics, fame
21 captured, seized
22 defended
23 likely, probably, perhaps
24 injury, damage★
25 although
26 nature
27 business, commerce

35   Most of our city did. Only myself stood out,[28]
     For which, if I be lapsèd[29] in this place,
     I shall pay dear.

Sebastian   Do not then walk too open.

Antonio   It doth not fit[30] me. Hold sir, here's my purse.
     In the south suburbs, at the Elephant,[31]
40   Is best to lodge. I will bespeak our diet,[32]
     Whiles you beguile[33] the time, and feed your knowledge
     With viewing of the town. There shall you have[34] me.

Sebastian   Why I your purse?

Antonio   Haply your eye shall light upon some toy[35]
45   You have desire to purchase. And your store[36]
     I think is not[37] for idle markets,[38] sir.

Sebastian   I'll be your purse-bearer and leave you
     For an hour.

Antonio   To th' Elephant.

Sebastian   I do remember.

EXEUNT

28 stood out = stayed out, did not participate
29 pounced upon
30 suit, seem proper/appropriate to
31 an inn
32 bespeak our diet = arrange our meals/food
33 wile away
34 find
35 trifle
36 stock of money
37 not sufficient to be expended
38 idle markets = frivolous/trifling buying

SCENE 4

Olivia's garden

ENTER OLIVIA AND MARIA

Olivia I have sent after him,[1] he says he'll come.
  How shall I feast him? What bestow of[2] him?
  For youth is bought more oft than begged or borrowed.
  I speak too loud.
  Where's Malvolio? He is sad and civil,[3]   5
  And suits well for a servant with my fortunes.
  Where is Malvolio?

Maria He's coming, madam. But in very strange manner. He
 is sure possessed,[4] madam.

Olivia Why, what's the matter, does he rave?   10

Maria No, madam, he does nothing but smile. Your ladyship
 were best to have some guard about you, if he come, for sure
 the man is tainted in's wits.

Olivia Go call him hither.

EXIT MARIA

      I am as mad as he,
 If sad and merry madness equal be.   15

ENTER MARIA, WITH MALVOLIO

 How now, Malvolio?

Malvolio Sweet lady, ho, ho.

Olivia Smilest thou?

1 after him = for him (i.e., Viola/Cesario)
2 on
3 sad and civil = steady/grave/serious and orderly/proper/decent
4 in the power of a demon/spirit

I sent for thee upon a sad occasion.[5]

20 *Malvolio* Sad lady, I could be sad. This does make some
obstruction in the blood, this cross-gartering, but what of
that? If it please the eye of one, it is with me as the very true
sonnet[6] is, "Please one, and please all."[7]

Olivia Why, how dost thou, man? What is the matter with
25 thee?

Malvolio Not black[8] in my mind, though yellow in my legs. It
did come to his hands, and commands shall be executed. I
think we do know the sweet Roman hand.[9]

Olivia Wilt thou go to bed, Malvolio?

30 *Malvolio* To bed? Ay, sweetheart, and I'll come to thee.

Olivia God comfort thee! Why dost thou smile so and kiss thy
hand so oft?

Maria How do you, Malvolio?

Malvolio (*to Maria? to Olivia?*) At your request. (*to Maria*) Yes,
35 nightingales answer daws.[10]

Maria Why appear you with this ridiculous boldness before
my lady?

Malvolio "Be not afraid of greatness." 'Twas well writ.

Olivia What meanest thou by that, Malvolio?

40 *Malvolio* "Some are born great" –

---

5 business, affair
6 song, lyric poem
7 "Please one and please all, / Be they great be they small, / Be they little be
   they low, / So pipeth the crow, / Sitting upon a wall. / Please one and please
   all. / Please one and please all" (1592: *Twelfe Night, or What You Will,* New
   Variorum ed., ed. Horace Howard Furness [Philadelphia: Lippincott, 1901],
   217–218)
8 malignant, disastrous, melancholy
9 i.e., round, bold handwriting
10 nightingales: Malvolio; daws (crows): Maria

Olivia	Ha!
Malvolio	"Some achieve greatness" –
Olivia	What sayest thou?
Malvolio	"And some have greatness thrust upon them."
Olivia	Heaven restore thee!

45

Malvolio	"Remember who commended thy yellow stockings" –
Olivia	Thy yellow stockings?
Malvolio	"And wished to see thee cross-gartered."
Olivia	Cross-gartered?
Malvolio	"Go to, thou art made, if thou desirest to be so" –

50

Olivia	Am I made?
Malvolio	"If not, let me see thee a servant still."
Olivia	Why, this is very midsummer[11] madness.

ENTER SERVANT

Servant	Madam, the young gentleman of the Count Orsino's is returned, I could hardly entreat him back.[12] He attends[13] your ladyship's pleasure.
Olivia	I'll come to him.

55

EXIT SERVANT

Good Maria, let this fellow[14] be looked to. Where's my cousin Toby? Let some of my people have a special care of him,[15] I would not have him miscarry[16] for the half of my dowry.

60

11 Midsummer Eve (23 June): the height of the lunacy (moon-derived) season
12 to come back
13 waits for★
14 Malvolio
15 Malvolio
16 come to harm

EXEUNT OLIVIA AND MARIA

Malvolio O ho, do you come near me[17] now? No worse man
than Sir Toby to look to me! This concurs[18] directly with the
letter, she sends him on purpose, that I may appear
65 stubborn[19] to him. For she incites me to that in the letter.
"Cast thy humble slough," says she. "Be opposite with a
kinsman, surly with servants, let thy tongue tang with
arguments of state, put thyself into the trick of singularity."
And consequently[20] sets down the manner how. As, a sad
70 face, a reverend carriage, a slow tongue, in the habit of some
sir[21] of note, and so forth. I have limed[22] her, but it is Jove's
doing, and Jove make me thankful! And when she went away
now,[23] "Let this fellow be looked to." Fellow? Not Malvolio,
nor after[24] my degree, but fellow. Why, everything adheres[25]
75 together, that[26] no dram[27] of a scruple, no scruple of a
scruple, no obstacle, no incredulous[28] or unsafe circumstance.
What can be said? Nothing that can be[29] can come between
me and the full prospect[30] of my hopes. Well, Jove, not I, is
the doer of this, and he is to be thanked.

17 come near me = get a clearer picture / understanding of me
18 converges, agrees, combines
19 (1) fierce, implacable, ruthless, (2) unyielding
20 thereafter
21 gentleman
22 caught (as birds were snared, with a sticky substance known as "bird-lime")
23 just now
24 according to
25 is attached
26 so that there is
27 a very small measure of weight
28 incredible, unbelievable
29 that can be = possible
30 outlook, future expectations

ENTER MARIA, WITH SIR TOBY AND FABIAN

Sir Toby   Which way[31] is he,[32] in the name of sanctity? If all the   80
devils of hell be drawn in little,[33] and Legion[34] himself
possessed him,[35] yet I'll speak to him.

Fabian   Here he is, here he is. How is't with you, sir? How is't
with you, man?

Malvolio   Go off,[36] I discard[37] you. Let me enjoy my private.[38]   85
Go off.

Maria   Lo, how hollow[39] the fiend speaks within him. Did not
I tell you? Sir Toby, my lady prays you to have a care of him.

Malvolio   Ah ha, does she so?

Sir Toby   (*to Fabian and Maria*) Go to, go to. Peace, peace, we must   90
deal gently with him. Let me alone. How do you, Malvolio?
How is't with you? What man, defy the devil. Consider, he's
an enemy to mankind.

Malvolio   Do you know what you say?

Maria   La you,[40] an you speak ill of the devil, how he takes it   95
at heart. Pray God, he be not bewitched.

Fabian   Carry his water[41] to th' wise woman.[42]

Maria   Marry, and it shall be done tomorrow morning, if I live.

---

31 which way = where ("what direction")
32 Malvolio
33 in little = on a small scale
34 a company of demons (biblical: see Mark 5:9)
35 Malvolio
36 away
37 reject, dismiss, banish
38 privacy
39 dismally, tomb-like
40 la you = exclamation of surprise
41 urine
42 wise woman = female magician, sorceress ("white witch")

My lady would not lose him for more than I'll say.

100 *Malvolio* How now, mistress?

Maria O Lord!

Sir Toby Prithee hold thy peace, this is not the way. Do you not see you move⁴³ him? Let me alone with him.

Fabian No way but gentleness, gently, gently. The fiend is
105 rough, and will not be roughly used.

Sir Toby Why how now, my bawcock?⁴⁴ How dost thou, chuck?⁴⁵

Malvolio Sir!

Sir Toby Ay, biddy,⁴⁶ come with me. What man, 'tis not for
110 gravity⁴⁷ to play at cherry-pit⁴⁸ with Satan. Hang⁴⁹ him, foul collier!⁵⁰

Maria Get him to say his prayers, good Sir Toby, get him to pray.

Malvolio My prayers, minx!⁵¹

115 *Maria* No, I warrant you, he will not hear of godliness.

Malvolio Go hang yourselves all! You are idle shallow things, I am not of your element,⁵² you shall know more hereafter.

EXIT MALVOLIO

Sir Toby Is't possible?

43 disturb, excite, stir up
44 fine fellow (BAWEcock)
45 familiar affectionate form of address
46 chick (usually used to women)
47 serious/important people
48 children's game, throwing cherry-pits into a hole in the ground
49 damn
50 coal dealer/merchant (blackened by trade)
51 hussy, wanton young woman
52 social community

Fabian   If this were played upon a stage now, I could
condemn it as an improbable fiction.[53]   120

Sir Toby   His very genius[54] hath taken the infection of the
device, man.

Maria   Nay, pursue him now, lest the device take air,[55] and
taint.

Fabian   Why, we shall make him mad indeed.   125

Maria   The house will be the quieter.

Sir Toby   Come, we'll have him in[56] a dark room and bound.
My niece is already in the belief that he's mad. We may carry
it[57] thus, for our pleasure and his penance, till our very
pastime, tired out of breath, prompt us to have mercy on him.   130
At which time we will bring the device to the bar[58] and
crown thee for a finder of madmen. But see, but see.

ENTER SIR ANDREW

Fabian   More matter for a May[59] morning.

Sir Andrew Here's the challenge, read it. I warrant there's vinegar
and pepper in't.   135

Fabian   Is't so saucy?

Sir Andrew Ay, is't? I warrant him.[60] Do but read.

Sir Toby   Give me. (*reading*) "Youth, whatsoever thou art, thou
art but a scurvy fellow."

53 invention
54 spirit, nature, character
55 take air = be exposed
56 put in
57 it on
58 to the bar = into court (the railing in front of the judge)
59 wild (as in May Day games)
60 it

140 *Fabian* Good, and valiant.

Sir Toby (*reading*) "Wonder not, nor admire[61] not in thy mind,
why I do call thee so, for I will show thee no reason for't."

Fabian A good note,[62] that keeps you from the blow[63] of the
law.

145 *Sir Toby* (*reading*) "Thou comst to the lady Olivia, and in my
sight she uses thee kindly, but thou liest in thy throat, that is
not the matter I challenge thee for."

Fabian Very brief, and to exceeding good sense – less.

Sir Toby (*reading*) "I will waylay thee going home, where if it be

150 thy chance to kill me" –

Fabian Good.

Sir Toby (*reading*) "Thou killest me like a rogue and a villain."

Fabian Still you keep o' the windy[64] side of the law. Good.

Sir Toby (*reading*) "Fare thee well, and God have mercy upon

155 one of our souls. He may have mercy upon mine, but my
hope[65] is better, and so look to thyself. Thy friend, as thou
usest him, and thy sworn enemy, ANDREW AGUECHEEK." If this
letter move him not, his legs cannot. I'll give't him.

Maria You may have very fit occasion for't. He is now in some

160 commerce[66] with my lady, and will by and by[67] depart.

Sir Toby Go, Sir Andrew. Scout me[68] for him at the corner of the
orchard like a bum-baily.[69] So soon as ever thou seest him,

61 be surprised
62 feature
63 application, shock, calamitous effect
64 (1) windward (i.e., facing/aware/mindful of the wind), (2) flatulent
65 expectation, desire
66 dealings, business, conversation
67 by and by = soon*
68 scout me = spy ("me" is reflexive and without any other meaning)
69 bum-baily = bailiff, sheriff's officer

draw; and as thou drawest swear horrible. For it comes to pass
oft, that a terrible oath, with a swaggering[70] accent sharply
twanged off,[71] gives manhood more approbation[72] than ever   165
proof[73] itself would have earned him.[74] Away!
Sir Andrew Nay, let me alone for swearing.

EXIT SIR ANDREW

Sir Toby   Now will not I deliver his letter. For the behavior of
the young gentleman gives him out to be of good capacity
and breeding. His employment between his lord and my   170
niece confirms no less. Therefore, this letter, being so
excellently ignorant, will breed no terror in the youth. He
will find[75] it comes from a clodpole.[76] But sir, I will deliver
his challenge by word of mouth, set[77] upon Aguecheek a
notable report of valor, and drive the gentleman (as I know   175
his youth will aptly receive it) into a most hideous[78] opinion
of his rage, skill, fury, and impetuosity.[79] This will so fright
them both that they will kill one another by the look, like
cockatrices.[80]

ENTER OLIVIA, WITH VIOLA

70 blustering, insolent★
71 twanged off = uttered
72 sanction, approval
73 demonstration
74 it (manhood)
75 perceive
76 blockhead
77 place, fix
78 frightful
79 violent energy
80 serpent capable of killing with a glance ("basilisk")

180 *Fabian* Here he comes with your niece. Give them way[81] till
he take leave, and presently after him.

Sir Toby I will meditate the while upon some horrid[82] message
for a challenge.

EXEUNT SIR TOBY, FABIAN, AND MARIA

Olivia I have said too much unto a heart of stone,
185 And laid mine honor too unchary on't.[83]
There's something in me that reproves my fault.
But such a headstrong potent[84] fault it is,
That it but mocks reproof.

Viola With the same 'havior that your passion bears,
190 Goes on[85] my master's griefs.

Olivia Here, wear this jewel for me, 'tis my picture.
Refuse it not, it hath no tongue to vex you.
And I beseech you come again tomorrow.
What shall[86] you ask of me that I'll deny,[87]
195 That honor (saved)[88] may upon asking give?

Viola Nothing but this, your true love for my master.

Olivia How with mine honor may I give him that
Which I have given to you?

Viola   I will acquit[89] you.

Olivia Well, come again tomorrow. Fare thee well.

---

81 give them way = stay at a distance from them
82 terrible, dreadful, frightful
83 unchary on't = incautiously on that heart
84 powerful
85 goes on = continues, persists
86 must, will
87 refuse★
88 except
89 discharge, release

A fiend like[90] thee might bear my soul to hell.   200

EXIT OLIVIA

ENTER SIR TOBY AND FABIAN

Sir Toby Gentleman, God save thee.

Viola   And you, sir.

Sir Toby That defense[91] thou hast, betake[92] thee to't. Of what
nature the wrongs are thou hast done him, I know not. But
thy intercepter, full of despite,[93] bloody as the hunter,   205
attends[94] thee at the orchard-end. Dismount thy tuck,[95] be
yare[96] in thy preparation, for thy assailant is quick, skillful, and
deadly.

Viola   You mistake sir I am sure, no man hath any quarrel to
me. My remembrance is very free and clear from any image   210
of offense done to any man.

Sir Toby You'll find it otherwise, I assure you. Therefore, if you
hold your life at any price, betake you to your guard.[97] For
your opposite hath in him what youth, strength, skill, and
wrath can furnish man withal.   215

Viola   I pray you sir, what is he?

Sir Toby He is knight dubbed,[98] with unhatched[99] rapier and on

90 resembling, who looked like
91 i.e., the sword that all gentlemen wore
92 entrust, commit★
93 disdain, scorn
94 waits for
95 dismount thy tuck = unsheath your sword/rapier
96 ready
97 protection, defense
98 sworn in, invested
99 unstained, unbloodied

carpet consideration,[100] but he is a devil in private brawl,[101] souls and bodies hath he divorced three, and his

220 incensement[102] at this moment is so implacable, that satisfaction[103] can be none, but[104] by pangs of death and sepulcher. Hob, nob[105] is his word. Give't or take't.

Viola   I will return again into the house, and desire some conduct of[106] the lady. I am no fighter. I have heard of some

225 kind of men, that put quarrels purposely on others, to taste their valor. Belike this is a man of that quirk.[107]

Sir Toby   Sir, no. His indignation derives itself[108] out of a very competent[109] injury, therefore get you on and give him his desire. Back you shall[110] not to the house, unless you

230 undertake that[111] with me,[112] which with as much safety you might answer him. Therefore on,[113] or strip your sword stark naked.[114] For meddle[115] you must, that's certain, or forswear to wear iron[116] about you.

100 on carpet consideration = knighted as a matter of court-procedures (as opposed to battlefield merit)
101 private brawl = personal quarrels
102 anger, wrath
103 solution, release ("payment of debt")
104 except
105 hob, nob = get it or give it
106 conduct of = escort from
107 peculiarity
108 derives itself = is caused by, comes from
109 (1) sufficient, (2) appropriate, proper
110 may, must
111 accept, do
112 in the dueling code, a man's second could if necessary / appropriate also demand the right to fight
113 proceed
114 strip your sword stark naked = completely divest yourself of your sword
115 fight
116 i.e., a sword

Viola   This is as uncivil as strange. I beseech you, do me this
courteous office,[117] as to know of[118] the knight what my   235
offense to him is. It is something of my negligence,[119]
nothing of my purpose.

Sir Toby   I will do so. Signior Fabian, stay you by this gentleman
till my return.[120]

EXIT SIR TOBY

Viola   Pray you sir, do you know of[121] this matter?   240

Fabian   I know the knight is incensed against you, even to a
mortal arbitrement,[122] but nothing of the circumstance
more.

Viola   I beseech you, what manner of man is he?

Fabian   Nothing of that wonderful promise, to read him by his   245
form,[123] as you are like to find him in the proof of his valor.
He is indeed sir, the most skillful, bloody, and fatal opposite
that you could possibly have found in any part of Illyria. Will
you walk towards him? I will make your peace with him if I
can.   250

Viola   I shall be much bound[124] to you for't. I am one that had
rather go with sir priest than sir knight. I care not who knows
so much of my mettle.[125]

---

117 service, kindness
118 know of = be informed by
119 carelessness, inattention
120 i.e., keep him from running away
121 about
122 decision, settlement
123 appearance ("body shape")
124 obliged
125 (1) temperament, spirit, (2) courage★

EXEUNT

ENTER SIR TOBY, WITH SIR ANDREW

Sir Toby   Why man, he's a very devil, I have not seen such a
255   firago.[126] I had a pass[127] with him – rapier, scabbard,[128] and
all – and he gives me the stuck in[129] with such a mortal
motion,[130] that it is inevitable. And on the answer, he pays[131]
you as surely[132] as your feet hit the ground they step on. They
say he has been fencer to the Sophy.

260 *Sir Andrew*   Pox on't, I'll not meddle with him.

Sir Toby   Ay, but he will not now be pacified. Fabian can
scarce hold him yonder.

Sir Andrew   Plague on't, and[133] I thought he had been valiant
and so cunning in fence,[134] I'ld have seen him damned ere
265   I'ld have challenged him. Let him let the matter slip, and I'll
give him my horse, gray Capilet.

Sir Toby   I'll make the motion.[135] Stand here, make a good
show on't. This shall end without the perdition of souls.
(*aside*) Marry, I'll ride your horse as well as I ride you.

ENTER FABIAN AND VIOLA

270   (*to Fabian*) I have his horse to take up[136] the quarrel, I have
persuaded him the youth's a devil.

126 warrior
127 bout, round
128 i.e., with the sword sheathed
129 stuck in = thrust, stab ("stoccado")
130 mortal motion = deadly thrust
131 punishes
132 certainly
133 if
134 fencing
135 proposal, suggestion
136 take up = buy up, lift, dissolve, check

Fabian   He[137] is as horribly conceited[138] of him,[139] and
pants and looks pale, as if a bear were at his heels.

Sir Toby   (*to Viola*) There's no remedy sir, he will fight with you
for 's oath sake. Marry, he hath better bethought him of[140] his   275
quarrel, and he finds that now scarce to be worth talking of.
Therefore draw, for the supportance[141] of his vow. He
protests he will not hurt you.

Viola   (*aside*) Pray God defend me! A little thing would
make me tell them how much I lack of[142] a man.   280

Fabian   Give ground, if you see him furious.[143]

Sir Toby   Come, Sir Andrew, there's no remedy, the gentleman
will, for his honor's sake have one bout with you. He cannot
by the duello[144] avoid it. But he has promised me, as he is a
gentleman and a soldier, he will not hurt you. Come on, to't.   285

Sir Andrew   Pray God, he keep his oath!

Viola   I do assure you, 'tis against my will.

THEY DRAW

ENTER ANTONIO

Antonio   Put up your sword. If this young gentleman
Have done offense, I take the fault on me.
If you offend him, I for him defy you.   290

Sir Toby   You, sir? Why, what are you?

137 Viola
138 as horribly conceited = has the same dreadful / frightful opinion
139 Sir Andrew
140 bethought him of = considered, reflected
141 support, upholding
142 of being
143 fiery, raging
144 dueling's establish code

Antonio	One sir, that for his love[145] dares yet do more
	Than you have heard him brag to you he will.
Sir Toby	Nay, if you be an undertaker,[146] I am for you.

THEY DRAW

ENTER OFFICERS

295	*Fabian*	O good Sir Toby, hold. Here come the officers.
	Sir Toby	(*to Antonio*) I'll be with you anon.[147]
	Viola	(*to Sir Andrew*) Pray sir, put your sword up, if you please.
	Sir Andrew	Marry will I, sir. And for[148] that I promised you, I'll be as good as my word. He will bear you easily and reins well.
300	*First Officer*	This is the man, do thy office.[149]
	Second Officer	Antonio, I arrest thee at the suit[150] of Count Orsino.
	Antonio	You do mistake me, sir.
	First Officer	No sir, no jot. I know your favor well, Though now you have no sea-cap on your head.
305		Take him away, he knows I know him well.
	Antonio	I must obey. (*to Viola*) This comes with[151] seeking you.
		But there's no remedy, I shall answer it.

145 for his love = on account of my love for him
146 someone who accepts a challenge
147 shortly, in a moment
148 as for
149 duty
150 at the suit = pursuant to the prosecution
151 from

What[152] will you do,[153] now[154] my necessity
Makes me to ask you for my purse? It grieves me
Much more for what I cannot do for you   310
Than what befalls myself. You stand amazed,
But be of comfort.

Second Officer   Come sir, away.

Antonio   I must entreat of you some of that money.

Viola   What money, sir?   315
For the fair[155] kindness you have showed me here,
And part[156] being prompted by your present trouble,
Out of my lean and low ability[157]
I'll lend you something. My having[158] is not much,
I'll make division of my present[159] with you.   320
Hold, there's half my coffer.[160]

Antonio   Will you deny[161] me now?
Is't possible that my deserts[162] to you
Can lack persuasion?[163] Do not tempt my misery,
Lest that it make me so unsound[164] a man
As to upbraid you with those kindnesses   325
That I have done for you.

152 how
153 manage, survive
154 now that
155 courteous
156 in part
157 capacity
158 property, possessions
159 what I now have
160 funds
161 repudiate, disown, reject
162 worthy conduct
163 belief, conviction
164 corrupt, insincere

Viola   I know of none,
    Nor know I you by voice, or any feature.[165]
    I hate ingratitude more in a man
    Than lying, vainness,[166] babbling, drunkenness,
330   Or any taint of vice whose strong corruption[167]
    Inhabits our frail blood.
Antonio   O heavens themselves!
Second Officer Come sir, I pray you go.
Antonio   Let me speak a little. This youth that you see here
    I snatched one half out of[168] the jaws of death,
335   Relieved him with such sanctity of love,[169]
    And to his image, which methought did promise
    Most venerable[170] worth, did I devotion.[171]
First Officer   What's that to us? The time goes by.[172] Away!
Antonio   But O how vile[173] an idol proves this god.
340   Thou hast, Sebastian, done good feature shame.[174]
    In nature there's no blemish but the mind.
    None can be called deformed but the unkind.[175]
    Virtue is beauty, but the beauteous evil[176]

---

165 aspect of appearance*
166 vanity
167 depravity, perversion
168 one half out of = when he was already halfway swallowed by death
169 such sanctity of love = just as much/the same amount of inviolable/
    absolute friendship/regard
170 highly respected
171 did I devotion = I was devoutly/earnestly/enthusiastically dedicated
172 goes by = is passing/slipping past
173 disgusting, despicable, degraded
174 done good feature shame = shamed handsome looks
175 (1) ungrateful, (2) unnatural
176 evil people

Are empty trunks[177] o'erflourished[178] by the devil.

First Officer   The man grows mad, away with him! Come, come,   345
sir.

Antonio   Lead me on.

EXIT ANTONIO WITH OFFICERS

Viola   Methinks his words do from such passion fly,
That he believes himself, so do not I.
Prove true imagination, O prove true,
That I dear brother, be now ta'en for you!   350

Sir Toby   Come hither knight, come hither Fabian. We'll
whisper o'er[179] a couplet[180] or two of most sage saws.[181]

Viola   He named Sebastian. I my brother know
Yet living in my glass.[182] Even such and so
In favor was my brother, and he went   355
Still[183] in this fashion,[184] color, ornament,[185]
For him I imitate.[186] O if it prove,[187]
Tempests are kind and salt waves fresh in love.

EXIT VIOLA

Sir Toby   A very dishonest paltry[188] boy, and more a coward

177 bodies
178 painted over
179 whisper o'er = speak softly/secretly, repeating
180 couplet = two-line rhyming form
181 most sage saws = exceedingly wise maxims/proverbs
182 mirror
183 always
184 shape ("fashioning")
185 luster, quality
186 reproduce, very closely resemble
187 is established/demonstrated
188 dishonest paltry = disgraceful/dishonorable contemptible/worthless/
    despicable

360 than a hare.[189] His dishonesty appears in leaving his friend
here in necessity and denying him. And for his cowardship,
ask Fabian.

Fabian   A coward, a most devout coward, religious in it.

Sir Andrew 'Slid,[190] I'll after him again and beat him.

365 *Sir Toby*   Do, cuff him soundly, but never draw thy sword.

Sir Andrew An I do not –

EXIT SIR ANDREW

Fabian   Come, let's see the event.[191]

Sir Toby   I dare lay[192] any money 'twill be nothing yet.[193]

EXEUNT

---

189 (?) merely someone who runs away
190 God's eyelid (mild curse)
191 what actually happens
192 wager, bet
193 still, again

Act 4

ENTER SEBASTIAN AND FESTE

Feste   Will you make me believe that I am not[1] sent for you?

Sebastian Go to, go to, thou art a foolish fellow.

Let me be clear[2] of thee.

Feste   Well held out,[3] i' faith! No, I do not know you, nor I
am not sent to you by my lady, to bid you come speak with   5
her, nor your name is not Master[4] Cesario, nor this is not my
nose neither. Nothing that is so, is so.

Sebastian I prithee, vent[5] thy folly somewhere else.

Thou know'st not me.

Feste   Vent my folly! He has heard that word of[6] some great   10

---

1 am not = have not been
2 free
3 held out = kept up, maintained, continued
4 form of address used primarily (though not exclusively) for young gentlemen
5 (1) sell, (2) spout, discharge, express
6 from

man and now applies it to a fool. Vent my folly! I am afraid
this great lubber,[7] the world, will prove a cockney.[8] I prithee
now, ungird[9] thy strangeness and tell me what I shall vent to
my lady. Shall I vent to her that thou art coming?

15 *Sebastian*   I prithee, foolish Greek,[10] depart from me.
There's money for thee. If you tarry longer,
I shall give worse payment.

Feste   By my troth, thou hast an open hand.[11] These wise
men that give fools money get themselves a good report[12] –
20 after fourteen years' purchase.[13]

ENTER SIR ANDREW, SIR TOBY, AND FABIAN

Sir Andrew Now sir, have I met you again? (*strikes Sebastian*)
There's for you.

Sebastian   (*beating Sir Andrew*) Why there's for thee, and there,
and there.

25 Are all the people mad?

Sir Toby   (*to Sebastian*) Hold sir, or I'll throw your dagger[14]
o'er the house.

Feste   This will I tell my lady straight.[15] I would not be in
some of your coats for two pence.

EXIT FESTE

7 clumsy fellow
8 pampered child, milksop, fop
9 free yourself from, drop
10 loose fellow, deceiving person
11 thou hast an open hand = you're generous/bounteous
12 name, reputation
13 of bringing it about (i.e., paying)
14 (?) with which, presumably still sheathed, Sebastian has been beating Sir
   Andrew
15 directly, at once

Sir Toby	(*grasping Sebastian*) Come on sir, hold.

         30

Sir Andrew Nay, let him alone, I'll go another way to work with him. I'll have an action of battery against him, if there be any law in Illyria. Though I stroke[16] him first, yet it's no matter for that.

Sebastian (*to Sir Toby*) Let go thy hand.   35

Sir Toby Come sir, I will not let you go. Come my young soldier, put up your iron. You are well fleshed.[17] Come on.

Sebastian I will be free from thee. (*draws his sword*) What wouldst thou now? If thou darest tempt me further, draw thy sword.   40

Sir Toby What, what? (*draws his sword*) Nay, then I must have an ounce or two of this malapert[18] blood from you.

ENTER OLIVIA

Olivia Hold Toby, on thy life I charge thee hold!

Sir Toby (*sheathing his sword*) Madam.

Olivia Will it be ever thus? Ungracious[19] wretch,   45
Fit for the mountains and the barbarous caves,
Where manners ne'er were preached! Out of my sight!
(*to Sebastian*) Be not offended, dear Cesario.
(*to Sir Toby*) Rudesby,[20] be gone!

EXEUNT SIR TOBY BELCH, SIR ANDREW, AND FABIAN

                                     I prithee, gentle friend,
Let thy fair wisdom, not thy passion, sway   50

16 struck
17 well fleshed = eager to fight
18 impudent, saucy
19 unmannerly
20 disorderly fellow, ruffian

In this uncivil and unjust extent[21]
Against thy peace. Go with me to my house,
And hear thou there how many fruitless pranks[22]
This ruffian hath botched up,[23] that thou thereby
55   Mayst smile at this. Thou shalt not choose but go.[24]
Do not deny.[25] Beshrew his soul for me,
He started[26] one poor heart[27] of mine in thee.[28]

Sebastian (*aside*) What relish[29] is in this? How runs the stream?[30]
Or[31] I am mad, or else this is a dream.
60   Let fancy still my sense[32] in Lethe[33] steep.[34]
If it be thus to dream, still[35] let me sleep.

Olivia   Nay come, I prithee. Would thou'st[36] be ruled[37] by me!

Sebastian Madam, I will.

Olivia   O say so, and so be!

EXEUNT

21 assault, attack
22 fruitless pranks = useless/idle/vain wicked tricks
23 botched up = patched together, contrived
24 come
25 say no
26 roused, frightened
27 i.e., the metaphor is from deer ("hart") hunting
28 in thee: in Elizabethan love language, the lover's heart is literally seized/captured by the belovèd, so that frightening Viola (which is who Olivia thinks that Sebastian is) frightens Olivia's heart, inside him
29 pleasure, zest
30 i.e., what is going on?
31 either
32 perception ("senses")
33 river in Hades, one sip of which caused complete forgetting (LEEthee)
34 still . . . steep = continue steeping/enveloping/bathing
35 always
36 would thou'st = I wish you would be
37 governed, led

SCENE 2

Olivia's house

ENTER MARIA AND FESTE

Maria   Nay, I prithee put on this gown[1] and this beard, make
him believe thou art Sir Topas[2] the curate, do it quickly. I'll
call Sir Toby the whilst.

EXIT MARIA

Feste   Well, I'll put it on, and I will dissemble[3] myself in't, and I
would I were the first that ever dissembled in such a gown. I   5
am not tall[4] enough to become the function[5] well, nor lean
enough to be thought a good student.[6] But to be said[7] an
honest[8] man and a good housekeeper[9] goes as fairly as to say
a careful[10] man and a great scholar. *The competitors[11] enter.*

ENTER SIR TOBY AND MARIA

Sir Toby   Jove bless thee, Master Parson.   10
Feste   *Bonos dies,*[12] Sir Toby. For as the old hermit of

1 clerical robes
2 a reference to Chaucer's self-parodistic "Sir Thopas," in *The Canterbury Tales*
3 disguise, deceive
4 (1) elegant, fine, (2) stout, (3) tall
5 activity
6 students were often extremely poor, as was the clerk/student in Chaucer's
   Canterbury Tales
7 to be said = to have it said that one is
8 respectable, honorable
9 hospitable householder
10 attentive, painstaking, heedful
11 the competitors = my associates
12 *bonos dies, = buenas dias,* "good day" (Spanish or, perhaps, bad Latin – in
   which language *salve* = good day)

Prague,[13] that never saw pen and ink, very wittily said to a
niece of King Gorboduc,[14] "That that is, is." So I being
Master Parson, am Master Parson. For what is "that" but
15 "that"? And "is" but "is"?

Sir Toby   To him,[15] Sir Topas.

Feste   What ho, I say! Peace[16] in this prison![17]

Sir Toby   The knave counterfeits[18] well. A good knave.

Malvolio   (*within*) Who calls there?

20 *Feste*   Sir Topas the curate, who comes to visit Malvolio the
lunatic.

Malvolio   Sir Topas, Sir Topas, good Sir Topas, go to my lady.

Feste   Out hyperbolical fiend,[19] how vexest thou this man!
Talkest thou nothing but of ladies?

25 *Sir Toby*   Well said, Master Parson.

Malvolio   Sir Topas, never was man thus wronged, good Sir Topas,
do not think I am mad. They have laid me here in hideous
darkness.

Feste   Fie, thou dishonest Satan! I call thee by the most
30 modest terms, for I am one of those gentle ones that will use
the devil himself with courtesy. Sayst thou that house[20] is
dark?

13 invented by Feste
14 early British king, celebrated in pre-Shakespearean drama
15 to him = at/attack him (often used to spur on hunting dogs)
16 quiet
17 i.e., as a clergyman, Sir Topas has become familiar with disorderly conditions
in the prisons of Elizabethan England – and Malvolio is effectively in a
prison
18 imitates
19 hyperbolical fiend = extravagant demon (i.e., a demon supposedly
possessing Malvolio)
20 place of abode/rest

Malvolio As hell, Sir Topas.

Feste   Why it hath bay windows transparent as barricadoes,[21]
and the clerestories[22] toward the south north are as lustrous[23]   35
as ebony. And yet complainest thou of obstruction?

Malvolio I am not mad Sir Topas, I say to you this house is dark.

Feste   Madman, thou errest.[24] I say there is no darkness but
ignorance, in which thou art more puzzled[25] than the
Egyptians in their fog.[26]   40

Malvolio I say this house is as dark as ignorance, though
ignorance were as dark as hell, and I say there was never man
thus abused. I am no more mad than you are, make the trial[27]
of it in any constant[28] question.

Feste   What is the opinion of Pythagoras[29] concerning wild   45
fowl?

Malvolio That the soul of our grandam[30] might haply inhabit a
bird.

Feste   What thinkst thou of his opinion?

Malvolio I think nobly of the soul, and no way approve[31] his   50
opinion.

Feste   Fare thee well. Remain thou still in darkness, thou

21 ramparts, barriers
22 rows of windows, high on a wall (KLIstereez)
23 glossy, shiny
24 have gone astray, are wrong
25 confused
26 a three-day "thick darkness" instigated at Moses' request (Exodus 10:21)
27 test
28 certain, fixed, unchanging
29 6th c. B.C.E. Greek philosopher, believer in the transmigration of souls
   (piTHAgorus)
30 grandmother
31 confirm, sanction

shalt³² hold the opinion of Pythagoras ere I will allow of³³

thy wits. And fear³⁴ to kill a woodcock, lest thou dispossess³⁵

55   the soul of thy grandam. Fare thee well.

Malvolio Sir Topas, Sir Topas!

Sir Toby (*aside*) My most exquisite³⁶ Sir Topas!

Feste   (*aside*) Nay, I am for all waters.³⁷

Maria   (*aside*) Thou mightst have done this without thy beard

60   and gown, he sees thee not.

Sir Toby (*aside*) To him in thine own voice, and bring me word

how thou findst him. I would we were well rid of this

knavery. If he may be conveniently delivered,³⁸ I would he

were, for I am now so far in offense with my niece, that I

65   cannot pursue with any safety this sport to the upshot. Come

by and by to my chamber.

EXEUNT SIR TOBY AND MARIA

Feste   (*singing*)

    Hey Robin, jolly Robin,

    Tell me how thy lady does.

70 *Malvolio* Fool!

Feste   (*singing*) My lady is unkind, perdy.³⁹

Malvolio Fool!

Feste   (*singing*) Alas, why is she so?

---

32 must
33 allow of = sanction, approve
34 you must be afraid
35 dislodge, drive out
36 ingenious, delicious, excellent
37 i.e., I go anywhere, tackle anything
38 freed
39 by God

Malvolio Fool, I say!

Feste   (*singing*) She loves another – Who calls, ha?   75

Malvolio Good fool, as ever[40] thou wilt deserve well at my hand,
      help me to a candle, and pen, ink, and paper. As I am a
      gentleman, I will live to be thankful to thee for't.

Feste   Master Malvolio?

Malvolio Ay, good fool.   80

Feste   Alas, sir, how fell you besides[41] your five wits?

Malvolio Fool, there was never a man so notoriously[42] abused. I
      am as well in my wits, fool, as thou art.

Feste   But as well? Then you are mad indeed, if you be no
      better in your wits than a fool.   85

Malvolio They have here propertied[43] me. Keep[44] me in
      darkness, send ministers[45] to me – asses! – and do all they can
      to face[46] me out of my wits.

Feste   Advise[47] you what you say; the minister is here.
      (*changing voice*) Malvolio, Malvolio, thy wits the heavens   90
      restore! Endeavor thyself to sleep, and leave thy vain[48] bibble
      babble.[49]

Malvolio Sir Topas.

Feste   (*as Sir Topas*) Maintain[50] no words with him, good

40 as ever = to the extent that
41 out of
42 obviously★
43 taken possession of
44 they keep
45 (1) agents, (2) clergymen
46 bully★
47 consider, watch
48 profitless, useless, worthless
49 bibble babble = prating, empty talk
50 carry on, keep up

95   fellow. (*Feste*) Who, I, sir? not I, sir. God be wi' you, good Sir
          Topas. (*Sir Topas*) Marry, amen.[51] (*Feste*) I will sir, I will.

      Malvolio Fool, fool, fool, I say!

      Feste   Alas sir, be patient. What say you sir? I am shent[52] for
      speaking to you.

100 *Malvolio* Good fool, help me to some light, and some paper, I
          tell thee, I am as well in my wits as any man in Illyria.

      Feste   Well-a-day,[53] that you were[54] sir.

      Malvolio By this hand I am. Good fool, some ink, paper, and
      light. And convey what I will set down to my lady. It shall
105   advantage thee more than ever the bearing of letter did.

      Feste   I will help you to't. But tell me true, are you not mad
      indeed, or do you but counterfeit?

      Malvolio Believe me, I am not, I tell thee true.

      Feste   Nay, I'll ne'er believe a madman till I see his brains. I
110   will fetch you light, and paper, and ink.

      Malvolio Fool, I'll requite it in the highest degree. I prithee be
      gone.[55]

      Feste   (*singing*)

          I am gone sir,

115   And anon sir,

            I'll be with you again,[56]

          In a trice,

          Like to the old Vice,[57]

---

51 may it be so
52 disgraced
53 O alas
54 that you were = if only you were
55 be gone = go and get it
56 pronounced, in England, aGAYN (rhyming with "pain," "main," etc.)
57 character in the old morality plays of the Middle Ages and early Renaissance

Your need to sustain.[58]

Who with dagger of lath,[59]   120
In his rage and his wrath,
   Cries ah ha, to the devil,
Like a mad lad,
Pare[60] thy nails,[61] dad,[62]
   Adieu good man devil.   125

EXIT FESTE

58 support
59 narrow strips of thin wood, nailed to a wall to hold plaster
60 trim
61 nails, claws
62 Vice was sometimes represented as the devil's son

SCENE 3

Olivia's garden

ENTER SEBASTIAN

Sebastian This is the air, that is the glorious sun,
This pearl she gave me, I do feel't and see't
And though 'tis wonder that enwraps me thus,
Yet 'tis not madness. Where's Antonio, then?
5   I could not find him at the Elephant,
Yet there he was,[1] and there I found this credit,[2]
That he did range[3] the town to seek me out.
His counsel now might do me golden service,
For though my soul disputes well with my sense
10   That this may be some error, but no madness,
Yet doth this accident and flood of fortune
So far exceed all instance,[4] all discourse,[5]
That I am ready to distrust mine eyes
And wrangle[6] with my reason that persuades me
15   To any other trust[7] but that I am mad,
Or else the lady's mad. Yet, if 'twere so,
She could not sway her house, command her followers,
Take, and give back affairs, and their dispatch,[8]
With such a smooth, discreet, and stable bearing

1 had been
2 report
3 roam
4 causation, logic
5 reasoning
6 dispute, argue
7 reliance, confident belief, hope
8 settlement, accomplishment, execution

As I perceive she does. There's something in't   20
That is deceiveable.[9] But here the lady comes.

ENTER OLIVIA AND PRIEST

Olivia   Blame[10] not this haste of mine. If you mean well,
    Now go with me and with this holy man
    Into the chantry by.[11] There before him,
    And underneath that consecrated roof,   25
    Plight[12] me the full assurance of your faith,
    That[13] my most jealous and too doubtful soul
    May live at peace. He[14] shall conceal it,
    Whiles[15] you are willing it shall come to note,
    What[16] time we will our celebration keep[17]   30
    According to my birth.[18] What do you say?
Sebastian I'll follow this good man, and go with you,
    And having sworn truth, ever will be true.
Olivia   Then lead the way good father, and heavens so shine,
    That they may fairly note this act of mine!   35

EXEUNT

9 deceptive, fallible
10 censure, find fault with
11 chantry by = chapel close by
12 pledge
13 so that
14 the priest
15 until
16 at which
17 celebration keep = wedding feast observe
18 according to my birth = in accord with my noble status

Act 5

SCENE I

In front of Olivia's house

ENTER FESTE AND FABIAN

Fabian Now, as thou lovst me, let me see his[1] letter.

Feste Good Master Fabian, grant me another[2] request.

Fabian Anything.

Feste Do not desire to see this letter.

5 *Fabian* This is, to give a dog, and in recompense desire my dog again.[3]

ENTER ORSINO, VIOLA, CURIO, AND LORDS

Orsino Belong you to the Lady Olivia, friends?

Feste Ay sir, we are some of her trappings.[4]

---

1 Malvolio's
2 a different
3 A courtier of Queen Elizabeth I had a dearly loved dog. The queen said that if he would give her the dog, she would give him anything he wanted. He gave her the dog and then, as his request, asked for the dog back.
4 ornaments, decorations

Orsino I know thee well. How dost thou, my good fellow?

Feste Truly sir, the better for my foes and the worse for my   10
friends.

Orsino Just the contrary; the better for thy friends.

Feste No sir, the worse.

Orsino How can that be?

Feste Marry sir, they praise me and make an ass of me. Now   15
my foes tell me plainly I am an ass. So that by my foes sir, I
profit in the knowledge of myself, and by my friends I am
abused. So that[5] conclusions to be as kisses, if your four[6]
negatives make your[7] two affirmatives,[8] why then the worse
for my friends, and the better for my foes.   20

Orsino Why, this is excellent.

Feste By my troth sir, no. Though it please you to be one of
my friends.

Orsino Thou shalt not be the worse for me, there's gold.

Feste But[9] that it would be double-dealing sir, I would you   25
could make it another.

Orsino O you give me ill counsel.

Feste Put your grace[10] in your pocket sir, for this once, and let
your flesh and blood obey it.

Orsino Well, I will be so much a sinner to be[11] a double-dealer.   30
There's another.

---

5 so that = so that if/in order that
6 if your four = if four
7 make your = make
8 two double negatives making one positive, four double negatives make two
affirmatives (logic chopping)
9 except
10 goodwill, liberality
11 to be = as to be

Feste   Primo, secundo, tertio,[12] is a good play,[13] and the old saying
          is, the third pays for all.[14] The triplex[15] sir, is a good tripping
          measure,[16] or the bells of Saint Bennet[17] sir, may put you in
35   mind – one, two, three.

Orsino   You can fool no more money out of me at this throw.[18]
         If you will let your lady know I am here to speak with her,
         and bring her along with you, it may awake my bounty
         further.

40   Feste   Marry sir, lullaby to your bounty till I come again. I go
          sir, but I would not have you to think that my desire of having
          is the sin of covetousness. But as you say sir, let your bounty
          take a nap, I will awake it anon.

EXIT FESTE

Viola   Here comes the man sir, that did rescue me.[19]

ENTER ANTONIO AND OFFICERS

45   Orsino   That face of his I do remember well,
          Yet when I saw it last, it was besmeared
          As black as Vulcan,[20] in the smoke of war.
          A bawbling[21] vessel was he captain of,
          For shallow draught and bulk unprizable,[22]

12 one, two, three (Latin)
13 a good play = good playing (in a children's dice game)
14 maxim: "The third pays [makes up] for all" (in throwing dice)
15 triple time (i.e., fast)
16 tripping measure = light-footed rhythm/tune
17 Benedict (a church near the Globe Theatre)
18 an allusion to throwing dice
19 i.e., in the brawl with Sir Andrew, *not* in the sea-wreck
20 Roman god of fire and metal-working
21 trifling, trivial, insignificant
22 not worth capturing as a prize

With which such scathful grapple[23] did he make,   50
With the most noble bottom[24] of our fleet,
That very[25] envy and the tongue of loss[26]
Cried[27] fame and honor on him. What's the matter?

First Officer Orsino, this is that Antonio
That took[28] the *Phoenix* and her fraught from Candy,[29]   55
And this is he that did the *Tiger* board,
When your young nephew Titus lost his leg.
Here in the streets, desperate[30] of shame and state,[31]
In private brabble[32] did we apprehend him.

Viola   He did me kindness sir, drew[33] on my side,   60
But in conclusion[34] put strange speech upon me,[35]
I know not what 'twas, but distraction.[36]

Orsino   Notable[37] pirate, thou salt-water thief,
What foolish boldness brought thee to their mercies,
Whom thou in terms so bloody, and so dear,[38]   65
Hast made thine enemies?

Antonio   Orsino. Noble sir,

23 scathful grapple = injurious/damaging fastening onto another boat
24 noble bottom = greatest/most splendid/magnificent ship
25 even
26 i.e., those who lost by his activity (the Illyrians)
27 pronounced, evoked, ordained
28 captured
29 her fraught from Candy = the *Phoenix*'s cargo, carried from Crete (*Phoenix:* an Illyrian ship)
30 reckless, indifferent to
31 (1) circumstances, (2) order, public peace, (3) the state ("country") he is in
32 private brabble = personal quarrel (of a paltry/noisy sort)
33 drew his sword
34 the end
35 put strange speech upon me = uttered/spoke odd words/strangely to me
36 mental/emotional disturbance
37 (1) conspicuous, easily noticed, (2) remarkable, excellent
38 costly, important

Be pleased[39] that I shake off these names you give me.
Antonio never yet was thief or pirate,
Though I confess, on base and ground[40] enough,
70   Orsino's enemy. A witchcraft drew me hither.
That most ingrateful boy there by your side,
From the rude sea's enraged and foamy mouth
Did I redeem. A wrack[41] past hope he was.
His life I gave him, and did thereto add
75   My love without retention, or restraint,[42]
All his in dedication. For his sake
Did I expose myself (pure[43] for his love)
Into the danger of this adverse[44] town,
Drew to defend him, when he was beset.[45]
80   Where being apprehended,[46] his false[47] cunning
(Not meaning to partake[48] with me in danger)
Taught him to face me out of his acquaintance,
And grew[49] a twenty years removèd[50] thing
While one would wink. Denied me mine own purse,
85   Which I had recommended[51] to his use
Not half an hour before.

39 contented, satisfied ("in good humor about")
40 base and ground = foundation and circumstance
41 shipwrecked/lost person
42 retention, or restraint = holding back, or reserve
43 purely
44 hostile
45 surrounded, attacked, assailed
46 where being apprehended = where I/Antonio was seized/arrested
47 lying, treacherous
48 share
49 became ("grew into")
50 distant
51 committed

Viola	How can this be?
Orsino	When came he to this town?

Antonio Today my lord. And for three months before,
No interim,[52] not a minute's vacancy,[53]
Both day and night did we keep company.   90

ENTER OLIVIA AND ATTENDANTS

Orsino Here comes the Countess, now heaven walks on earth.
But for[54] thee fellow: fellow, thy words are madness,
Three months this youth hath tended[55] upon me.
But more of that anon. Take him aside.

Olivia What would my lord, but[56] that he may not have,   95
Wherein Olivia may seem serviceable?[57]
Cesario, you do not keep promise with me.

Viola Madam –

Orsino Gracious Olivia –

Olivia What do you say, Cesario? Good my lord –   100

Viola My lord would speak, my duty hushes me.

Olivia If it be aught to the old tune my lord,
It is as fat and fulsome[58] to mine ear
As howling after music.

Orsino	Still so cruel?

Olivia Still so constant, lord.   105

Orsino What, to perverseness?[59] You uncivil lady,

52 intervening time
53 cease, absence
54 as for
55 attended
56 but that = except that which
57 ready to be of service
58 fat and fulsome = heavy and rank / over-grown
59 stubbornness, wrongheadedness

To whose ingrate and unauspicious[60] altars
My soul the faithfull'st offerings hath breathed out
That e'er devotion tendered! What shall I do?

110 *Olivia* Even[61] what it please my lord, that shall become him.

Orsino Why should I not, had I the heart to do it,
Like to th' Egyptian thief at point of death,
Kill what I love?[62] (A savage jealousy
That sometimes savors[63] nobly.) But hear me this.

115 Since you to non-regardance[64] cast my faith,
And that I partly know the instrument
That screws[65] me from my true place in your favor,
Live you the marble-breasted[66] tyrant still.
But this your minion,[67] whom I know you love,

120 And whom, by heaven I swear, I tender[68] dearly,
Him will I tear out of that cruel eye,
Where he sits crownèd in his master's spite.
Come boy with me, my thoughts are ripe in mischief.[69]
I'll sacrifice the lamb that I do love,

125 To spite a raven's heart within a dove.

Viola And I, most jocund,[70] apt, and willingly,
To do you rest, a thousand deaths would die.

---

60 unfavorable, unkind
61 exactly
62 as in Heliodorus's *Aethiopica*, a Greek novel from ca. 300 C.E., in which a
   besieged bandit tries to kill his dearly loved female captive
63 pleases
64 that which is beneath regard / notice
65 forces, presses
66 i.e., with a heart as cold as marble
67 darling
68 regard
69 evil, harm
70 cheerful, merry

Olivia   Where goes Cesario?
Viola   After him I love
     More than I love these eyes, more than my life,
     More, by all mores, than e'er I shall love wife.   130
     If I do feign, you witnesses above
     Punish my life for tainting of my love.
Olivia   Ay me detested, how am I beguiled![71]
Viola   Who does beguile you? Who does do you wrong?
Olivia   Hast thou forgot thyself? Is it so long?   135
     Call forth the holy father.
Orsino   Come, away!
Olivia   Whither my lord? Cesario, husband, stay.
Orsino   Husband?
Olivia   Ay husband. Can he that deny?
Orsino   Her husband, sirrah?[72]
Viola   No my lord, not I.
Olivia   Alas, it is the baseness[73] of thy fear   140
     That makes thee strangle thy propriety.[74]
     Fear not Cesario, take thy fortunes up,[75]
     Be that thou know'st thou art, and then thou art
     As great as that[76] thou fear'st.

ENTER PRIEST

                              O welcome, father!
     Father, I charge thee by thy reverence[77]   145

71 deceived, cheated
72 term of address, spoken to persons below the speaker in status
73 meanness, lowliness
74 own nature/essence
75 take thy fortunes up = claim/accept your good luck
76 that which
77 sacred/exalted character

Here to unfold, though lately we intended
To keep in darkness, what occasion now
Reveals before 'tis[78] ripe: what thou dost know
Hath newly passed between this youth and me.

150 *Priest*   A contract of eternal bond of love,
Confirmed by mutual joinder of your hands,
Attested by the holy close[79] of lips,
Strengthened by interchangement of your rings,
And all the ceremony of this compact
155   Sealed in my function,[80] by my testimony.
Since when, my watch hath told me, toward my grave
I have traveled but two hours.

  Orsino (*to Viola*) O thou dissembling[81] cub! What wilt thou be
When time hath sowed a grizzle on thy case?[82]
160   Or will not else thy craft[83] so quickly grow,
That thine own trip[84] shall be thine overthrow?
Farewell, and take her, but direct thy feet
Where thou and I henceforth may never meet.

  Viola   My lord, I do protest –
  Olivia   O do not swear!
165   Hold little[85] faith, though thou hast too much fear.

ENTER SIR ANDREW

78 'tis = the time is
79 joining (in a kiss)
80 in my function = by my performance/activity/powers
81 hypocritical
82 grizzle on thy case = gray hair on your exterior
83 cunning, dexterity, skill
84 tripping of somebody else
85 hold little = keep a little

Sir Andrew For the love of God a surgeon,[86] send one presently
to Sir Toby.

Olivia   What's the matter?

Sir Andrew H'as broke[87] my head across,[88] and has given Sir
Toby a bloody coxcomb[89] too. For the love of God your help,   170
I had rather than forty pound[90] I were at home.[91]

Olivia   Who has done this, Sir Andrew?

Sir Andrew The Count's gentleman, one Cesario. We took him
for a coward, but he's the very devil incardinate.[92]

Orsino   My gentleman Cesario?   175

Sir Andrew 'Od's lifelings,[93] here he is! You broke my head for
nothing, and that that I did, I was set on to do't by Sir Toby.

Viola   Why do you speak to me, I never hurt you.
You drew your sword upon me without cause,
But I bespake you[94] fair, and hurt you not.   180

Sir Andrew If a bloody coxcomb be a hurt, you have hurt me. I
think you set[95] nothing by a bloody coxcomb.

ENTER SIR TOBY AND FESTE

Here comes Sir Toby halting,[96] you shall hear more. But if he
had not been in drink, he would have tickled you

86 doctor
87 he has wounded
88 from one side to the other
89 top of the head
90 rather than forty pound = even more than I would like to have 40 pounds
91 i.e., in the country
92 incarnate
93 'Od's lifelings = by God's own life
94 bespake you = spoke to you
95 allot, give, place
96 limping

185   othergates[97] than he did.

Orsino   How now gentleman? How is't with you?

Sir Toby   That's all one, ha's[98] hurt me, and there's th' end on't.
    Sot, didst see Dick Surgeon, sot?

Feste   O he's drunk Sir Toby, an hour agone.[99] His eyes
190   were set[100] at eight i' the morning.

Sir Toby   Then he's a rogue, and a passy-measures pavin.[101] I
    hate a drunken rogue.

Olivia   Away with him! Who hath made this havoc[102] with
    them?

195   Sir Andrew   I'll help you Sir Toby, because we'll be dressed[103]
    together.

Sir Toby   Will you[104] help? An ass-head, and a coxcomb, and a
    knave, a thin-faced[105] knave, a gull?

Olivia   Get him to bed, and let his hurt be looked to.

EXEUNT FESTE, FABIAN, SIR TOBY, AND SIR ANDREW

ENTER SEBASTIAN

200   Sebastian   I am sorry madam I have hurt your kinsman,
    But had it been the brother of my blood,
    I must have done no less with[106] wit and safety.
    You throw a strange regard upon me, and by that

97 differently
98 he has
99 ago
100 closed, shut
101 i.e., *passamezzo pavana*, a pavan (slow and stately eight-bar dance)
102 devastation
103 fixed up, treated
104 will you = you want to
105 weak-faced
106 in, according to

I do perceive it hath offended you.

Pardon me, sweet one, even[107] for the vows   205

We made each other but so late ago.

Orsino   One face, one voice, one habit, and two persons,

A natural perspective,[108] that is, and is not.

Sebastian Antonio, O my dear Antonio!

How have the hours racked and tortured me,   210

Since I have lost thee!

Antonio   Sebastian are you?

Sebastian Fear'st thou[109] that, Antonio?

Antonio   How have you made division of yourself?

An apple, cleft in two, is not more twin

Than these two creatures. Which is Sebastian?   215

Olivia   Most wonderful.[110]

Sebastian Do I stand there? I never had a brother,

Nor can there be that deity[111] in my nature

Of[112] here and every where. I had a sister,

Whom the blind[113] waves and surges have devoured.   220

Of charity,[114] what kin are you to me?

What countryman?[115] What name? What parentage?

Viola   Of Messaline.[116] Sebastian was my father,

---

107 precisely
108 sight produced by a distorting mirror
109 fear'st thou = do you doubt
110 astonishing
111 divine quality
112 of being
113 unfeeling, uncaring, unknowing
114 i.e., in the name of Christian caring ("*caritas*")
115 what countryman = a man of/from what country
116 no such place exists or to my knowledge ever has existed. There is Messina,
   in Italy; there was Messene (meSEEN), in ancient Greece

Such[117] a Sebastian was my brother too.

225   So went he suited[118] to his watery tomb.

If spirits can assume both form and suit

You come to fright us.

Sebastian   A spirit[119] I am indeed,

But am in that dimension[120] grossly[121] clad

Which from the womb I did participate.[122]

230   Were you a woman, as the rest goes even,[123]

I should my tears let fall upon your cheek,

And say, "Thrice-welcome, drownèd Viola!"[124]

Viola   My father had a mole upon his brow.[125]

Sebastian And so had mine.

235 *Viola*   And died that[126] day when Viola from her birth

Had numbered thirteen years.

Sebastian O that record is lively in my soul,

He finished indeed his mortal act[127]

That day that made my sister thirteen years.

240 *Viola*   If nothing lets[128] to make us happy both

But this my masculine usurped attire,

Do not embrace me till each circumstance

117 similarly
118 so went he suited = wearing/bearing that name he went
119 soul
120 aspect, attribute
121 materially (as opposed to spiritually)
122 possess, have
123 the rest goes even = as all the other details point toward/indicate
124 and SAY thrice WELcome DROWNedVEEohLA
125 forehead
126 on that
127 state
128 hinders, obstructs, prevents

Of place, time, fortune, do cohere and jump[129]
That I am Viola, which to confirm,
I'll bring you to a captain in this town,   245
Where lie my maiden weeds.[130] By whose gentle help
I was preserved to serve this noble Count.
All the occurrence of my fortune[131] since
Hath been between this lady, and this lord.
Sebastian (*to Olivia*) So comes it, lady, you have been mistook.   250
But nature to her bias drew in[132] that.
You would have been contracted to a maid,
Nor are you therein (by my life) deceived,
You are betrothed[133] both to a maid and man.[134]
Orsino   Be not amazed, right noble is his blood.   255
If this be so, as yet the glass[135] seems true,
I shall have share in this most happy wreck.
(*to Viola*) Boy, thou hast said to me a thousand times
Thou never shouldst love woman like to[136] me.
Viola   And all those sayings will I overswear,[137]   260
And those swearings keep as true in soul
As doth that orbèd continent,[138] the fire
That severs day from night.

129 cohere and jump = fit together and coincide/agree exactly (of PLACE
     time FORtune DO coHERE and JUMP)
130 clothes
131 the occurrence of my fortune = that has happened to me
132 her bias drew in = her set course/predisposition pulled back
133 pledged, engaged
134 maid and man = virginal woman and virginal man
135 (?) (1) lens/optical aid (spy-glass, etc.), (2) mirror, (3) crystal (crystal ball?),
     (4) pane of glass covering a picture
136 like to = as you do
137 swear again
138 orbèd continent = circular mass (i.e., the sun)

Orsino   Give me thy hand,
          And let me see thee in thy woman's weeds.
265 *Viola*   The captain that did bring me first on shore
          Hath my maid's garments. He upon some action[139]
          Is now in durance,[140] at Malvolio's suit –
          A gentleman, and follower of my lady's.
     Olivia He shall enlarge[141] him. Fetch Malvolio hither –
270   And yet alas, now I remember me,
          They say poor gentleman, he's much distract.

               ENTER FESTE WITH A LETTER, AND FABIAN

          A most extracting frenzy[142] of mine own
          From my remembrance clearly banished his.
          How does he, sirrah?
275 *Feste*   Truly madam, he holds Belzebub[143] at the stave's end[144]
          as well as a man in his case may do. Has[145] here writ a letter
          to you. I should have given't you today morning.[146] But as a
          madman's epistles are no gospels,[147] so it skills not[148] much
          when they are delivered.
280 *Olivia* Open't, and read it.[149]
     Feste   Look then to be well edified[150] when the fool

139 legal proceeding
140 prison
141 release, set free
142 extracting frenzy = distracting excitement, agitation
143 the devil
144 at the stave's end = a stick-length away ("at a distance")
145 he has
146 today morning = this morning
147 biblical texts
148 makes no difference, does not matter
149 read it aloud
150 strengthened, informed

delivers[151] the madman. (*reading*) "By the Lord madam"[152] –

Olivia How now, art thou mad?

Feste   No madam, I do but read madness. And[153] your ladyship
will have it as it ought to be, you must allow vox.[154]   285

Olivia Prithee, read i' thy right wits.

Feste   So I do, madonna. But to read his[155] right wits is to read
thus.[156] Therefore perpend,[157] my princess, and give ear.

Olivia (*to Fabian*) Read it you, sirrah.

Fabian (*reading*) "By the Lord, madam, you wrong me, and the   290
world shall know it. Though you have put me into darkness,
and given your drunken cousin rule over me, yet have I the
benefit of my senses as well as[158] your ladyship. I have your
own letter that induced me to the semblance I put on, with
the which I doubt not but to do myself much right, or you   295
much shame. Think of me as you please. I leave my duty a
little unthought of and speak out of my injury.

THE MADLY-USED MALVOLIO."

Olivia Did he write this?

Feste   Ay, madam.   300

Orsino This savors not much of distraction.

Olivia See him delivered Fabian, bring him hither.

EXIT FABIAN

151 brings forth, presents, speaks for
152 i.e., by Mrs. God
153 if
154 voice ("the correct tone")
155 Malvolio's
156 the way I did
157 consider
158 as does

My lord so please you, these things further thought on,[159]

To[160] think me as well a sister as a wife,

305   One day shall crown[161] th' alliance on't,[162] so please you,

Here at my house and at my proper[163] cost.

Orsino   Madam, I am most apt to embrace your offer.

(to Viola) Your master quits[164] you. And for your service done him,

So much against the mettle[165] of your sex,

310   So far beneath your soft and tender breeding,

And since you called me master for so long,

Here is my hand. You shall from this time be

Your master's mistress.[166]

Olivia   A sister,[167] you are she!

ENTER FABIAN, WITH MALVOLIO

Orsino   Is this the madman?

Olivia   Ay my lord, this same.

How now, Malvolio?

315 Malvolio   Madam, you have done me wrong,

Notorious wrong.

Olivia   Have I Malvolio? No.

Malvolio   Lady you have, pray you peruse that letter.

You must not now deny it is your hand,

159 thought on = considered
160 in order to
161 complete, add the finishing touch to
162 alliance on't = kinship of it
163 own
164 releases (i.e., from the obligations of a servant)
165 temperament, spirit
166 Mrs.
167 a sister = I have a sister

Write from[168] it, if you can, in hand or phrase,

Or say 'tis not your seal, nor your invention.   320

You can say none of this. Well, grant[169] it then,

And tell me, in the modesty of honor,

Why you have given me such clear lights[170] of favor,

Bade me come smiling and cross-gartered to you,

To put on yellow stockings and to frown   325

Upon Sir Toby and the lighter[171] people.

And acting[172] this in an obedient hope,

Why have you suffered[173] me to be imprisoned,

Kept in a dark house, visited by the priest,

And made the most notorious geck[174] and gull   330

That e'er invention played on? Tell me why.

Olivia Alas Malvolio, this is not my writing,

Though I confess much like the character.[175]

But out of question 'tis Maria's hand.

And now I do bethink me, it was she   335

First told me thou wast mad, then cam'st[176] in smiling,

And in such forms,[177] which here were presupposed[178]

Upon thee in the letter. Prithee be content.

This practice hath most shrewdly passed[179] upon thee.

168 differently from
169 confess, admit, allow
170 suggestions
171 less important / significant
172 performing
173 tolerated, allowed
174 deceived / mocked person
175 style, handwriting
176 you came
177 arrangements, appearances, models
178 required, imposed
179 shrewdly passed = mischievously / naughtily imposed

340 But when we know the grounds and authors of it,
Thou shalt be both the plaintiff and the judge
Of thine own cause.

Fabian   Good madam hear me speak,
And let no quarrel nor no brawl to come
Taint the condition[180] of this present hour,
345 Which I have wondered at. In hope it shall not,
Most freely I confess myself and Toby
Set this device against Malvolio here,
Upon some stubborn[181] and uncourteous parts[182]
We had conceived[183] against him. Maria writ
350 The letter, at Sir Toby's great importance,[184]
In recompense whereof he hath married her.
How with a sportful malice[185] it was followed,[186]
May rather pluck[187] on laughter than revenge,
If that the injuries be justly weighed
355 That have on both sides passed.

Olivia (*to Malvolio*) Alas, poor fool, how have they baffled[188]
thee!

Feste   Why, "some are born great, some achieve greatness, and
some have greatness thrown upon them." I was one sir, in this
360 interlude,[189] one Sir Topas sir, but that's all one. "By the Lord

180 circumstances, state
181 unpleasantly inflexible
182 conduct, characteristics
183 formed, developed ("thought up")
184 solicitude, urging
185 sportful malice = frolicking/playful/entertaining mischievousness
186 carried out
187 bring
188 hoodwinked
189 little comedy

fool, I am not mad." But do you remember: "Madam, why
laugh you at such a barren rascal? And[190] you smile not, he's
gagged." And thus the whirligig[191] of time brings in his
revenges.

Malvolio   I'll be revenged on the whole pack of you.   365

EXIT MALVOLIO

Olivia   He hath been most notoriously abused.
Orsino   Pursue him and entreat[192] him to a peace.
   He hath not told us of the captain yet.
   When that is known, and golden time convents,[193]
   A solemn combination[194] shall be made   370
   Of our dear souls. Meantime, sweet sister,
   We will not part from hence. Cesario come –
   For so you shall be while you are a man,
   But when in other habits you are seen,
   Orsino's mistress, and his fancy's queen.   375

EXEUNT ALL, EXCEPT FESTE

Feste   (singing)
      When that I was and[195] a little tiny boy,
         With hey, ho, the wind and the rain,
      A foolish thing was but a toy
         For the rain it raineth every day.   380

190 if
191 spinning merry-go-round
192 negotiate
193 summons, calls together
194 joining
195 but

But when I came to man's estate,
    With hey, ho, the wind and the rain,
'Gainst knaves and thieves men shut their gate,[196]
    For the rain it raineth every day.

385 But when I came alas to wive,[197]
    With hey, ho, the wind and the rain,
By swaggering could I never thrive,[198]
    For the rain it raineth every day.

But when I came unto my beds,[199]
390   With hey, ho, the wind and the rain,
With[200] toss-pots[201] still had drunken heads,
    For the rain it raineth every day.

A great while ago the world begun,
    Hey, ho, the wind and the rain,
395 But that's all one, our play is done,
    And we'll strive to please you every day.

EXIT FESTE

196 (?) foolish things are not jokes/trifles to adults
197 marry
198 prosper
199 marriage beds? old age?
200 (?) just as? when?
201 drunkards

Clearly a kind of farewell to unmixed comedy, *Twelfth Night* nevertheless seems to me much the funniest of Shakespeare's plays, though I have yet to see it staged in a way consonant with its full humor. As some critics have noted, only Feste the clown among all its characters is essentially sane, and even he allows himself to be dragged into the tormenting of the wretched Malvolio, whose only culpability is that he finds himself in the wrong play, as little at home there as Shylock is in Venice.

Everything about *Twelfth Night* is unsettling, except for Feste again, and even he might be happier in a different play. Perhaps *Twelfth Night* was Shakespeare's practical joke upon his audience, turning all of them into Malvolios. Like *Measure for Measure,* the play would be perfectly rancid if it took itself seriously, which it wisely refuses to do. *Twelfth Night,* I would suggest, is a highly deliberate outrage, and should be played as such. Except for Feste, yet once more, none of its characters ought to be portrayed wholly sympathetically, not even Viola, who is herself a kind of passive zany, since who else would fall in love with the self-intoxicated Orsino?

What is most outrageous about *Twelfth Night* is Shakespeare's deliberate self-parody, which mocks his own originality at representation and thus savages representation or aesthetic imitation itself. Nothing happens in *Twelfth Night,* so there is no action to imitate anyway; *The Tempest* at least represents its opening storm, but *Twelfth Night* shrugs off its own, as if to say perfunctorily: let's get started. The shrug is palpable enough when we first meet Viola, at the start of scene 2:

> *Viola*   What country, friends, is this?
> *Captain* This is Illyria, lady.
> *Viola*   And what should I do in Illyria?
>   My brother he is in Elysium.
>   Perchance he is not drowned. What think you sailors?
>
>   [1.2.1–5]

Illyria is a kind of madcap Elysium, as we have discovered already, if we have listened intently to the superbly eloquent and quite crazy opening speech of its Duke:

> If music be the food of love, play on,
> Give me excess of it, that surfeiting,
> The appetite may sicken, and so die.
> That strain again, it had a dying fall.
> O it came o'er my ear, like the sweet sound
> That breathes upon a bank of violets,
> Stealing and giving odor. Enough, no more,
> 'Tis not so sweet now as it was before.
> O spirit of love, how quick and fresh art thou,
> That notwithstanding thy capacity
> Receiveth as the sea, nought enters there,

Of what validity and pitch soe'er,
But falls into abatement and low price,
Even in a minute. So full of shapes is fancy
That it alone is high fantastical.

[1.1.1–15]

Shakespeare himself so liked Orsino's opening conceit that he returned to it five years later in *Antony and Cleopatra* where Cleopatra, missing Antony, commands: "Give me some music; music, moody food / Of us that trade in love." Orsino, not a trader in love but a glutton for the idea of it, is rather more like John Keats than he is like Cleopatra, and his beautiful opening speech is inevitably echoed in Keats's "Ode on Melancholy." We can call Orsino a Keats gone bad, or even a little mad, returning us again to the mad behavior of nearly everyone in *Twelfth Night*. Dr. Samuel Johnson, who feared madness, liked to attribute rational design even where it seems unlikely: "Viola seems to have formed a very deep design with very little premeditation: she is thrown by shipwreck on an unknown coast, hears that the prince is a batchelor, and resolves to supplant the lady whom he courts."

Anne Barton more accurately gives us a very different Viola, whose "boy's disguise operates not as a liberation but merely as a way of going underground in a difficult situation." Even that seems to me rather more rational than the play's Viola, who never does come up from underground, but, then, except for Feste, who does? Feste surely speaks the play's only wisdom: "And thus the whirligig of time brings in his revenges" (5.1.364–65). "Time is a child playing draughts; the lordship is to the child" is the dark wisdom of Heracleitus. Nietzsche, with some desperation, had his Zarathustra proclaim the will's revenge against time, and in particular against time's assertion "It was." Shakespeare's time plays with a spinning top, so that time's revenges presumably have a circular aspect. Yet Feste sings that when he was a young fool, he was taken as a toy, certainly not the way we take him now. He knows what most critics of Shakespeare will not learn, which is that *Twelfth Night* does not come to any true resolution, in which anyone has learned anything. Malvolio might be an exemplary figure if we could smuggle him into a play by Ben Jonson, but *Twelfth Night,* as John Hollander long ago noted, appears to be a deliberately anti-Jonsonian drama. No one could or should be made better by viewing or reading it.

If it has no moral coherence, where then shall its coherence be found? Orsino, baffled by the first joint appearance of the twins Viola and Sebastian, is driven to a famous outburst:

One face, one voice, one habit, and two persons,
A natural perspective, that is, and is not.

[5.1.207–8]

Anne Barton glosses this as an optical illusion naturally produced, rather than given by a distorting perspective glass. Dr. Johnson gives the same reading rather more severely: "that nature has here exhibited such a show, where shadows seem realities; where that which 'is not' appears like that which 'is.'" A natural perspective is in this sense oxymoronic, unless time and nature are taken as identical, so that time's whirligig then would become the same toy as the distorting glass. If we could imagine a distorting mirror whirling in circles like a top, we would have the compound toy that *Twelfth Night* constituted for Shakespeare. Reflections in that mirror are the representations in *Twelfth Night*: Viola, Olivia, Sir Toby and Sir Andrew, Orsino, Sebastian, and all the rest except for Malvolio and Feste.

It is difficult for me to see Malvolio as an anti-Puritan satire, because Sir Toby, Sir Andrew, and Maria are figures even more unattractive, by any imaginative standards. Sir Toby is not a Falstaffian personage, no matter what critics have said. Falstaff without preternatural wit is not Falstaff, and Belch is just that: belch, rather than cakes and ale. Malvolio is an instance of a character who gets away even from Shakespeare, another hobgoblin run off with the garland of Apollo, like Shylock or like both Angelo and Barnardine in *Measure for Measure*. The relations between Ben Jonson and Shakespeare must have been lively, complex, and mutually ambivalent, and Malvolio seems to me Shakespeare's slyest thrust at Jonsonian dramatic morality. But even as we laugh at Malvolio's fall, a laughter akin to the savage merriment doubtless provoked in the Elizabethan audience by the fall of Shylock, so we are made uneasy at the fate of Malvolio and Shylock alike. Something in us rightly shudders when we are confronted by the vision of poor Malvolio bound in the dark room. An uncanny cognitive music emerges in the dialogue between Feste, playing Sir Topas the curate, and "Malvolio the lunatic":

Malvolio Sir Topas, Sir Topas, good Sir Topas, go to my lady.
Feste   Out hyperbolical fiend, how vexest thou this man! Talkest thou nothing but of ladies?
Sir Toby Well said, Master Parson.
Malvolio Sir Topas, never was man thus wronged, good Sir Topas, do not think I am mad. They have laid me here in hideous darkness.
Feste   Fie, thou dishonest Satan! I call thee by the most modest terms, for I am one of those gentle ones that will use the devil himself with courtesy. Sayst thou that house is dark?
Malvolio As hell, Sir Topas.

Feste   Why it hath bay windows transparent as barricadoes, and the clerestories toward the south north are as lustrous as ebony. And yet complainest thou of obstruction?

Malvolio I am not mad Sir Topas, I say to you this house is dark.

Feste   Madman, thou errest. I say there is no darkness but ignorance, in which thou art more puzzled than the Egyptians in their fog.

Malvolio I say this house is as dark as ignorance, though ignorance were as dark as hell, and I say there was never man thus abused. I am no more mad than you are, make the trial of it in any constant question.

Feste   What is the opinion of Pythagoras concerning wild fowl?

Malvolio That the soul of our grandam might haply inhabit a bird.

Feste   What thinkst thou of his opinion?

Malvolio I think nobly of the soul, and no way approve his opinion.

Feste   Fare thee well. Remain thou still in darkness, thou shalt hold the opinion of Pythagoras ere I will allow of thy wits. And fear to kill a woodcock, lest thou dispossess the soul of thy grandam. Fare thee well.

Malvolio Sir Topas, Sir Topas!

[4.2.22–56]

We are almost in the cosmos of *King Lear,* in Lear's wild dialogues with Edgar and Gloucester. Feste is sublimely wise, warning Malvolio against the ignorance of his Jonsonian moral pugnacity, which can make one as stupid as a woodcock. But there is a weirder cognitive warning in Feste's Pythagorian wisdom.

Metempsychosis or the instability of identity is the essence of
Twelfth Night, the lesson that none of its characters are capable of
learning, except for Feste, who learns it better all the time, even as
the whirligig of time brings in his revenges:

A great while ago the world begun,
    Hey, ho, the wind and the rain,
But that's all one, our play is done,
    And we'll strive to please you every day.

[5.1.393–96]

FURTHER READING

This is not a bibliography but a selective set of starting places.

Texts

Shakespeare, William. *The First Folio of Shakespeare,* 2d ed. Edited by
    Charlton Hinman. Introduction by Peter W. M. Blayney. New York:
    W. W. Norton, 1996.

Language

Dobson, E. J. *English Pronunciation, 1500–1700.* 2d ed. Oxford: Oxford
    University Press, 1968.
Houston, John Porter. *The Rhetoric of Poetry in the Renaissance and
    Seventeenth Century.* Baton Rouge: Louisiana State University Press,
    1983.
————. *Shakespearean Sentences: A Study in Style and Syntax.* Baton
    Rouge: Louisiana State University Press, 1988.
Kermode, Frank. *Shakespeare's Language.* New York: Farrar, Straus and
    Giroux, 2000.
Kökeritz, Helge. *Shakespeare's Pronunciation.* New Haven: Yale
    University Press, 1953.
Lanham, Richard A. *The Motives of Eloquence: Literary Rhetoric in the
    Renaissance.* New Haven and London: Yale University Press, 1976.
The Oxford English Dictionary: Second Edition on CD-ROM, version 3.0.
    New York: Oxford University Press, 2002.

Raffel, Burton. *From Stress to Stress: An Autobiography of English Prosody.* Hamden, Conn.: Archon Books, 1992.

Ronberg, Gert. *A Way with Words: The Language of English Renaissance Literature.* London: Arnold, 1992.

Trousdale, Marion. *Shakespeare and the Rhetoricians.* Chapel Hill: University of North Carolina Press, 1982.

Culture

Bindoff, S. T. *Tudor England.* Baltimore: Penguin, 1950.

Bradbrook, M. C. *Shakespeare: The Poet in His World.* New York: Columbia University Press, 1978.

Brown, Cedric C., ed. *Patronage, Politics, and Literary Tradition in England, 1558–1658.* Detroit, Mich.: Wayne State University Press, 1993.

Bush, Douglas. *Prefaces to Renaissance Literature.* New York: W. W. Norton, 1965.

Buxton, John. *Elizabethan Taste.* London: Harvester, 1963.

Cowan, Alexander. *Urban Europe, 1500–1700.* New York: Oxford University Press, 1998.

Driver, Tom E. *The Sense of History in Greek and Shakespearean Drama.* New York: Columbia University Press, 1960.

Finucci, Valeria, and Regina Schwartz, eds. *Desire in the Renaissance: Psychoanalysis and Literature.* Princeton, N.J.: Princeton University Press, 1994.

Fumerton, Patricia, and Simon Hunt, eds. *Renaissance Culture and the Everyday.* Philadelphia: University of Pennsylvania Press, 1999.

Halliday, F. E. *Shakespeare in His Age.* South Brunswick, N.J.: Yoseloff, 1965.

Harrison, G. B., ed. *The Elizabethan Journals: Being a Record of Those Things Most Talked of During the Years 1591–1597.* Abridged ed. 2 vols. New York: Doubleday Anchor, 1965.

Harrison, William. *The Description of England: The Classic Contemporary [1577] Account of Tudor Social Life.* Edited by Georges Edelen. Washington, D.C.: Folger Shakespeare Library, 1968. Reprint, New York: Dover, 1994.

Jardine, Lisa. "Introduction." In Jardine, *Reading Shakespeare Historically.* London: Routledge, 1996.

————. *Worldly Goods: A New History of the Renaissance*. London: Macmillan, 1996.

Jeanneret, Michel. *A Feast of Words: Banquets and Table Talk in the Renaissance*. Translated by Jeremy Whiteley and Emma Hughes. Chicago: University of Chicago Press, 1991.

Kernan, Alvin. *Shakespeare, the King's Playwright: Theater in the Stuart Court, 1603–1613*. New Haven: Yale University Press, 1995.

Lockyer, Roger. *Tudor and Stuart Britain, 1471–1714*. London: Longmans, 1964.

Norwich, John Julius. *Shakespeare's Kings: The Great Plays and the History of England in the Middle Ages, 1337–1485*. New York: Scribner, 2000.

Rose, Mary Beth, ed. *Renaissance Drama as Cultural History: Essays from Renaissance Drama, 1977–1987*. Evanston, Ill.: Northwestern University Press, 1990.

Schmidgall, Gary. *Shakespeare and the Courtly Aesthetic*. Berkeley: University of California Press, 1981.

Smith, G. Gergory, ed. *Elizabethan Critical Essays*. 2 vols. Oxford: Clarendon Press, 1904.

Tillyard, E. M. W. *The Elizabethan World Picture*. London: Chatto and Windus, 1943. Reprint, Harmondsworth: Penguin, 1963.

Willey, Basil. *The Seventeenth Century Background: Studies in the Thought of the Age in Relation to Poetry and Religion*. New York: Columbia University Press, 1933. Reprint, New York: Doubleday, 1955.

Wilson, F. P. *The Plague in Shakespeare's London*. 2d ed. Oxford: Oxford University Press, 1963.

Wilson, John Dover. *Life in Shakespeare's England: A Book of Elizabethan Prose*. 2d ed. Cambridge: Cambridge University Press, 1913. Reprint, Harmondsworth: Penguin, 1944.

Zimmerman, Susan, and Ronald F. E. Weissman, eds. *Urban Life in the Renaissance*. Newark: University of Delaware Press, 1989.

Dramatic Development

Cohen, Walter. *Drama of a Nation: Public Theater in Renaissance England and Spain*. Ithaca, N.Y.: Cornell University Press, 1985.

Dessen, Alan C. *Shakespeare and the Late Moral Plays*. Lincoln: University of Nebraska Press, 1986.

Fraser, Russell A., and Norman Rabkin, eds. *Drama of the English Renaissance.* 2 vols. Upper Saddle River, N.J.: Prentice Hall, 1976.

Happé, Peter, ed. *Tudor Interludes.* Harmondsworth: Penguin, 1972.

Laroque, François. *Shakespeare's Festive World: Elizabethan Seasonal Entertainment and the Professional Stage.* Translated by Janet Lloyd. Cambridge: Cambridge University Press, 1991.

Norland, Howard B. *Drama in Early Tudor Britain, 1485–1558.* Lincoln: University of Nebraska Press, 1995.

Theater and Stage

Doran, Madeleine. *Endeavors of Art: A Study of Form in Elizabethan Drama.* Milwaukee: University of Wisconsin Press, 1954.

Grene, David. *The Actor in History: Studies in Shakespearean Stage Poetry.* University Park: Pennsylvania State University Press, 1988.

Gurr, Andrew. *Playgoing in Shakespeare's London.* Cambridge: Cambridge University Press, 1987.

———. *The Shakespearian Stage, 1574–1642.* 3d ed. Cambridge: Cambridge University Press, 1992.

Halliday, F. E. *A Shakespeare Companion, 1564–1964.* Rev. ed. Harmondsworth: Penguin, 1964.

Harrison, G. B. *Elizabethan Plays and Players.* Ann Arbor: University of Michigan Press, 1956.

Holmes, Martin. *Shakespeare and His Players.* New York: Scribner, 1972.

Hotson, Leslie. *The First Night of "Twelfth Night."* New York: Macmillan, 1954.

Ingram, William. *The Business of Playing: The Beginnings of the Adult Professional Theater in Elizabethan London.* Ithaca, N.Y.: Cornell University Press, 1992.

Lamb, Charles. *The Complete Works and Letters of Charles Lamb.* Edited by Saxe Commins. New York: Modern Library, 1935.

LeWinter, Oswald, ed. *Shakespeare in Europe.* Cleveland, Ohio: Meridian, 1963.

Marcus, Leah S. *Unediting the Renaissance: Shakespeare, Marlowe, Milton.* London: Routledge, 1996.

Orgel, Stephen. *The Authentic Shakespeare, and Other Problems of the Early Modern Stage.* New York: Routledge, 2002.

Salgado, Gamini. *Eyewitnesses of Shakespeare: First Hand Accounts of Performances, 1590–1890*. New York: Barnes and Noble, 1975.

Stern, Tiffany. *Rehearsal from Shakespeare to Sheridan*. Oxford: Clarendon Press, 2000.

Thomson, Peter. *Shakespeare's Professional Career*. Cambridge: Cambridge University Press, 1992.

Webster, Margaret. *Shakespeare without Tears*. New York: Whittlesey House, 1942.

Weimann, Robert. *Shakespeare and the Popular Tradition in the Theater: Studies in the Social Dimension of Dramatic Form and Function*. Edited by Robert Schwartz. Baltimore: Johns Hopkins University Press, 1978.

Wikander, Matthew H. *The Play of Truth and State: Historical Drama from Shakespeare to Brecht*. Baltimore: Johns Hopkins University Press, 1986.

Yachnin, Paul. *Stage-Wrights: Shakespeare, Jonson, Middleton, and the Making of Theatrical Value*. Philadelphia: University of Pennsylvania Press, 1997.

Biography

Halliday, F. E. *The Life of Shakespeare*. Rev. ed. London: Duckworth, 1964.

Honigmann, F. A. J. *Shakespeare: The "Lost Years."* 2d ed. Manchester: Manchester University Press, 1998.

Schoenbaum, Samuel. *Shakespeare's Lives*. New ed. Oxford: Clarendon Press, 1991.

———. *William Shakespeare: A Compact Documentary Life*. Oxford: Oxford University Press, 1977.

General

Bergeron, David M., and Geraldo U. de Sousa. *Shakespeare: A Study and Research Guide*. 3d ed. Lawrence: University of Kansas Press, 1995.

Berryman, John. *Berryman's Shakespeare*. Edited by John Haffenden. Preface by Robert Giroux. New York: Farrar, Straus and Giroux, 1999.

Bradby, Anne, ed. *Shakespearian Criticism, 1919–35.* London: Oxford University Press, 1936.

Colie, Rosalie L. *Shakespeare's Living Art.* Princeton, N.J.: Princeton University Press, 1974.

Dean, Leonard F., ed. *Shakespeare: Modern Essays in Criticism.* Rev. ed. New York: Oxford University Press, 1967.

Goddard, Harold C. *The Meaning of Shakespeare.* 2 vols. Chicago: University of Chicago Press, 1951.

Kaufmann, Ralph J. *Elizabethan Drama: Modern Essays in Criticism.* New York: Oxford University Press, 1961.

McDonald, Russ. *The Bedford Companion to Shakespeare: An Introduction with Documents.* Boston: Bedford, 1996.

Raffel, Burton. *How to Read a Poem.* New York: Meridian, 1984.

Ricks, Christopher, ed. *English Drama to 1710.* Rev. ed. Harmondsworth: Sphere, 1987.

Siegel, Paul N., ed. *His Infinite Variety: Major Shakespearean Criticism Since Johnson.* Philadelphia: Lippincott, 1964.

Sweeting, Elizabeth J. *Early Tudor Criticism: Linguistic and Literary.* Oxford: Blackwell, 1940.

Van Doren, Mark. *Shakespeare.* New York: Holt, 1939.

Weiss, Theodore. *The Breath of Clowns and Kings: Shakespeare's Early Comedies and Histories.* New York: Atheneum, 1971.

Wells, Stanley, ed. *The Cambridge Companion to Shakespeare Studies,* Cambridge, Cambridge University Press, 1986.

FINDING LIST

Repeated unfamiliar words and meanings, alphabetically arranged, with act, scene, and footnote number of first occurrence, in the spelling (form) of that first occurrence

abuse (verb)	3.1.55	*cast*	1.5.106
admirable	2.3.51	*con*	1.5.107
affair	1.4.30	*crave*	2.1.4
alone	2.3.88	*cunning*	1.5.168
amend	1.5.28	*curtain*	1.3.69
answer	1.5.104	*defy*	1.5.83
apt	1.4.29	*degree*	1.3.58
assurance	1.5.115	*deliver*	1.5.141
attends	3.4.13	*demure*	2.5.41
bear-baiting	1.3.47	*deny*	3.4.87
befall	3.3.6	*desperate*	2.2.4
beshrew (verb)	2.3.50	*device*	2.3.107
bestowed	1.3.45	*disposition*	1.5.60
betake	3.4.92	*entertainment*	1.5.151
by and by	3.4.67	*envy*	2.1.27
capacity	2.5.76	*estate*	1.2.31

sot	1.5.81	*very*	1.2.19
state	1.5.194	*warrant* (verb)	2.3.110
swaggering	3.4.70	*way*	1.5.133
sway	2.4.20	*welkin*	2.3.29
taint (verb)	3.1.30	*wench*	1.3.24
taste (verb)	3.1.37	*wit*	1.2.51
troth	1.3.3	*woodcock*	2.5.57
uncivil	2.3.78	*yield*	3.1.13
usurp	1.5.120		